While the Blanket Is Short, Learn To Curl Up

While the Blanket Is Short, Learn To Curl Up

Michael C. Hawkins

Plain View Press
http://plainviewpress.net

3800 N. Lamar, Suite 730-260
Austin, TX 78756

ISBN: 978-1-935514-91-6
Library of Congress Control Number: 2011945371

Cover art: Untitled watercolor by Vicente Manansala.
Special thanks to Roberto Nolasco and Kulay-Diwa Gallery of Philippine Contemporary Art for the acquisition and use of this image. http://www.kulay-diwa.com/
Cover design by Pam Knight

Para sa mga Pilipino,
kahit saan man sa mundo

Contents

"Every moment in your life is a turning and every one a choosing. Somewhere you made a choice. All followed to this. The accounting is scrupulous. The shape is drawn. No line can be erased."

Cormac McCarthy
No Country for Old Men

Prologue

There is an old tale that circulates in certain portions of the Philippines that speaks of three men—a Spaniard, an American, and a Filipino—stranded together on a remote beach with no apparent escape. Their situation, as the story goes, became even more precarious as a typhoon bore down on them, bringing with it floods, waves, and inevitable death by drowning. Upon realizing the gravity of their circumstance, the Spaniard announced that he would pray to the Virgin Mother for salvation from the flood, and if this blessing was not to be, then he hoped for salvation in the life to come. And so, in his faith and fatalism the Spaniard knelt upon the sand and prayed fervently with rosary in hand for deliverance, contented with whatever outcome his fate had in store.

The American scoffed at this and looked around at his surroundings. After several seconds of observation he determined with certainty that he would fell trees, collect branches, perform various calculations and form a makeshift raft to deliver him from the flood. And if the raft should fail, he would swim with all his might until his strength was gone and the life was wrenched violently from his body. And so, in his determination and apparent exceptionalism the American set about breaking trees, collecting limbs, and making various measurements and computations that would save him from the coming catastrophe;

contented in his knowledge, ingenuity, and ability that he could determine the outcome and bend nature to his will.

As the two men sought out their respective salvations they noticed that the Filipino stood solemnly, mute as a stone staring off over the ocean into the gathering redness. They watched him, and he watched the sea. The Spaniard queried as to why he foolishly stood there, but there was no reply. The American pressed further and asked him if he had a plan, for his raft could not carry two and self-reliance was a virtue; but still the Filipino remained silent and the storm gathered in fury. The Spaniard prayed more fervently and the American worked more feverishly until the storm was finally upon them. As sheets of rain began to pock the sea at a near distance the American, with conflicted concern coloring his countenance, asked one final time what the Filipino planned to do. The native turned with a melancholy expression and offered a half smile. He regarded the American and then declared, "What can I do? I suppose I shall have to learn to live under water." And he turned back to face the tempest once again, contented in his ability to adapt and survive, knowing that no hardship or calamity was beyond his capacity to bear. And the storms came.

Cold, exposed the child wakes, the night has grown most black
Warmth and comfort do still escape, from his circumstance of lack
"Mother I am cold" he cries, and then comes the soft retort
"You must simply learn to curl up my son, while the blanket's short"

Michael Hawkins
July, 2011

Party at Auntie Vergie's

Marcus shuffled, dragging his feet to the rear passenger door of a faded blue Chevy Cavalier. "Come on *anak*. Get in," his mother urged, opening the car door. "You like it at Aunte Virgie's house, remember?"

Marcus slid to the center of the back seat without speaking and strapped the lap belt across his legs. His mother opened her own door and settled into the driver's seat. She sat up tall, looking for Marcus's face in the rearview mirror. "You used to love to go to these things. What happened?"

Marcus shrugged.

His mother studied the broken cement walkway leading to their half of an old dilapidated duplex. "They just give us so much support, *anak*. It's nice to connect with other Filipinos."

Marcus's face softened. "I know Mama." He offered a sympathetic smile but it faded quickly.

As the old Cavalier wound through the streets of their San Jose suburb Marcus contemplated his mother's words. It had been just the two of them now for almost two years. That didn't bother Marcus, though. He liked it better this way. He had only tolerated Jeff for his mother's sake. Jeff's aloof attitude and condescending tone was a constant reminder that he was not Marcus's father and never would be. His mother knew it wasn't an ideal situation, but it was better than starving to death in Tondo. Jeff sold pharmaceuticals. Marcus supposed this was why he had so many faces—friendly, angry, disgusted, apathetic, euphoric, and on and on. You have to adapt and mirror to be a good salesman. Or maybe he didn't know who he really was at all and so he tried on emotions and personalities at home like trying on new clothes. Whatever the reason Marcus's mother stood by him without complaint.

After their first year of marriage she pleaded with Jeff to help her petition her son in the Philippines. Jeff agreed to sign the necessary papers, but did little else. "If you want him here, you have to work it out," was all he said. She took a part-time job at a family video store for $7.50 an hour to cover the fees and solicited help from other Filipinos to organize the immigration forms. Eighteen months later, her petition was approved and Marcus arrived in San Jose three weeks after his ninth birthday.

Jeff welcomed him by rustling his thick black hair, but nothing else. Six months later, Jeff was gone. Maybe he resented the lavish attention Marcus received from his mother. Maybe he got just bored. Either way, one day out of the blue he announced that he had sold the house and wanted a divorce. Marcus's mother was shocked, but felt no pain. She nodded silently and began gathering her things. Though she accepted two hundred dollars a month in alimony, she didn't really want anything more from Jeff. She had what she needed now.

The pair moved into a shabby duplex for seven hundred dollars a month. Marcus Americanized quickly, losing his accent and adopting his friends' styles, diets, music tastes, and interests. Being foreign was not unique in this part of San Jose, but you didn't want to look foreign for very long. Marcus endured at least six months of being called "FOB" (fresh off the boat). Most of it was good natured, but much of it stung, especially from the Filipino and Vietnamese kids. As Marcus shed his foreign tendencies and began to look and act like the hyphenated Americans in his school, he sensed a gap developing between him and his mother. She seemed older, more inscrutable somehow, and at times inadequate. He felt as if he were being carried away on a conveyor belt while she remained still. He was passing her by into a cultural world she would never fully know or understand, and nothing could change that.

"They're going to sing today, you know." She smiled at him in the rearview mirror. "If you sing, '*I got a Feelin*' by the Black Eyed Peas, I'll sing the 'woo-hoo' part for you."

Marcus forced a chuckle. "Maybe."

"If you do, I'll sing '*I Cried a Tear.*'"

Marcus didn't answer.

She searched for his face in the mirror, though it was right in front of her. "All right then, it's a deal," she said. She liked the sound of that phrase; something distinctly American about it. It felt like real communication with her son; maybe something a cool mom would say. She had given up speaking Tagalog to Marcus, though he understood it perfectly, and now only spoke to him in a broken, constantly-evolving English, with mixed-up gender pronouns and sparing verb agreement.

After several minutes, the blue Cavalier pulled to a stop in front of a red brick single-story house. It was an older home, built in the 1950s. The wooden shingles had long ago turned dull gray and the grass was the color the shingles should have been, but other than that the house was neatly kept. Mother and son stepped out and walked to the door together. Auntie Vergie answered after only one knock. She was about ten years older than Marcus's mother, with short bobbed hair and large thighs. The two women embraced and smiled and spoke rapidly in their native tongue while Marcus lingered back, stuffing his hands in the pockets of his San Francisco 49ers hoody.

"*Ay, Dios ko*!" Vergie exclaimed. "Who is this handsome young man? It can't be Marcus."

Marcus fidgeted and smiled shyly and then looked away.

Vergie didn't wait for a response. "Give your Auntie Vergie a hug *hijo*!" She smothered the boy in a powerful embrace and kissed his neck twice. "You'll never outgrow your Auntie Vergie!"

Both women laughed and Marcus knit his brow.

Inside, the party was already well underway. Marcus sniffed the air. The most defining aspect of any Filipino party is always the smell; intoxicating to those who know it, and repugnant to those who don't. For Marcus it was sublime. Dark Silver Swan soy sauce, Datu Puti sugar cane vinegar, the citrusy tang of calamansi juice mixed with the pungent, sour smell of fish sauce and fermented shrimp paste danced around him, blending with the aroma of boiled crabs. His mouth watered at the barbeque pork skewers and pieces of fried chicken piled on a large serving platter. He surveyed the neatly-cut squares of sticky rice and snuck a piece of macaroni salad. He had come to realize that this was one thing his American friends would never understand, but on this particular issue he didn't care.

"Hi Marcus." A small girlish voice wafted in from behind him.

Marcus turned. "Oh, hi Sunshine."

The girl beamed. Though her given name was Victoria, family and friend simply called her Sunshine. She was Auntie Vergie's only child and an ideal model of the mixed-race features that Filipinos so covet—olive skin, hazel eyes, and light brown hair that turns rust color in the sun. "I'm glad you could come," she said, splitting her pony tail in two and tugging on each side to tighten the band. "Mama made pork barbeque because she knows you love it."

Marcus nodded but said nothing in response.

Sunshine coughed and looked away. "The kids are eating in the basement. Do you want to come down?"

Marcus thought for a moment and then shook his head. "No thanks. I think I'll stay up here for a while, but maybe I'll come down later."

Sunshine stared, confused by his reticence. "Ok," she said finally, and then bobbed her head awkwardly and turned toward the darkened door frame leading to the basement. Marcus pursed his lips and watched her disappear down the stairs.

He took a plate and filled it with all his favorites and sat down on a loveseat next to a window. Many of the Filipinas had already begun singing. English songs quickly gave way to Tagalog, and more and more joined in. Marcus sat back and closed his eyes as he listed to the familiar strains of Sharon Cuneta, Jaya, and Jessa Zaragosa. He did miss the Philippines. Things were better here in the United States, but not everything. He took a bite of pork barbeque and imagined he was passing the time with his cousins on the ashen gray streets of Tondo.

Sunshine's father sat down in a recliner next to the loveseat and pulled up the footrest. His plate was overflowing. Marcus quietly alternated his gaze between the man's plate and his stomach, trying to comprehend the size of each. He was an enormous man, from Swedish ancestry they said. Marcus didn't know where that was, but he concluded that they must be large people. The man wore a baggy Hawaiian style shirt and a pair of khaki shorts and nothing on his feet. Vergie remarked in Tagalog that it made him feel more Filipino to wear it. She rolled her eyes and shook her head. The other Filipinas giggled.

"How are you, boy?" The enormous man leaned toward the loveseat.

"I'm fine, thank you."

He shoveled in a mouthful of macaroni salad. "Sunshine sure was excited to hear you were coming."

Marcus took a drink of Sprite. "Oh."

"You know, I went to Tondo once on my way to Divisoria." He frowned. "Can't say that I cared for it much. Too much filth and poverty, even for the Philippines."

Marcus nodded but immediately regretted doing so.

The fat man went back to his plate. "I bet you're glad to be here."

Marcus didn't answer. He finished his rice and took the paper plate to a trash can, and then returned to the loveseat and sat with his hands in his front pocket. He looked around at this makeshift Filipino environment. There was so much about it that was familiar and so much that was strange and unsettling. The Filipinas were now up dancing. Vergie's husband struck up a conversation with two other Americans sitting on wooden chairs. They looked bored and anxious to leave. Marcus studied the contrast between the two groups.

"Pssst!"

Marcus looked toward the basement door. Another mixed-race girl about a year younger than he peeked out of the door frame. She waved him over. Marcus remained still.

"Come here," she urged. Marcus shook his head.

The girl looked behind her down the stairs momentarily, as if receiving instructions, and then waved at Marcus again. Still he didn't move. The girl sighed deeply in exasperation and dashed quietly behind the love seat.

"Psst!"

Marcus leaned over the back. "What?"

"Come downstairs." The girl smiled mischievously.

Marcus shook his head. "Not right now. Maybe later."

The girl looked to the stairs and then back again as if debating what to say next. "Sunshine wants you to come down." Marcus cocked an eyebrow. The girl was encouraged. "She likes you, you know. Why are you avoiding her?"

Marcus's mind cycled quickly. He considered the possibility that this might be some horrible trick meant to embarrass him. But on the other hand.... He waited and bit his lip and glanced back toward the stairs, and then looked over at Sunshine's father. He was regaling the two men with tales from his latest adventures in the Philippines, but heard nothing of the girl's pronouncements. Auntie Vergie was singing along with the chorus of "*Dahil ba sa kanya.*" Marcus leaned back. "Ok, tell her I'll be down in a minute." The girl giggled and ran back to the basement.

Marcus breathed deeply and tried to calm the butterflies in his stomach. He recalled and weighed each one of the girl's words. He replayed his conversation with Sunshine earlier as well. She was such a beautiful girl; so fair, so American, so unlike his mother. He imagined what his friends in the Philippines would say if they saw him with a girl like Sunshine; the jealous looks mingled with admiration, the fawning comments about her American features. The more he thought of it, however, the more the whole thing struck him as unexpectedly and inexplicably odd. He looked back at Sunshine's father. The large man was smiling and shaking his head. He said something about "not worth shitting on" and let out a guffaw. The other two men laughed as well. Marcus considered them for a long while. What did these Filipina women see in their husbands anyway? Their middle-age graying hair and potbellies, so unlike the robust American men in the movies. What did his mom ever see in Jeff? He watched the Filipinas dancing and singing in front of the television. They were so full of life and youth. Their eyes shined and their laughter came easy. A part of them so long suppressed around their husbands came bubbling to the top. He observed his mother thoughtfully. She looked different than the person he knew somehow, and more like someone he used to know. He watched her black hair sway back and forth and studied her smile. She was beautiful in a way he had not previously perceived. She was young and capable. She was Filipino like him; someone who understood him in a way no one else could; someone he could rely on. Something jerked in his throat and tears welled up in his eyes. He swallowed hard.

"Psst!" The same little girl as before appeared in the doorway. She scowled at Marcus and waved him over.

Marcus stood and walked across the living room to the basement door. "Tell her I'm not coming down. I promised my mother I'd sing with her today." The little girl looked confused. Marcus nodded sharply and then turned and walked over to the group of Filipinas. "Do you want to sing '*Tonight's Gonna be a Good Night*' with me Mama?" Marcus's mother stared in disbelief and then smiled and nodded, moved by his simple offer.

Auntie Vergie handed her the silver electronic mic and she punched in the appropriate numbers. The TV screen blipped blue and then transitioned to a tropical scene with swaying palm trees and a white beach lined with wooden lounge chairs. The music began. It was a pulsating beat with simple electronic notes. The screen counted down from three. Marcus put his mouth close to the mic. "*I got a feeling.*"

His mother leaned in "*Woo hoo.*"

"*That tonight's gonna be a good night, that tonight's gonna be a good good night…*" He sang joyfully and without inhibition. He and his mother breathed life into each other as the music created a world of rhythm and harmony. She watched her son throughout the song, not wanting the moment to pass. This little boy she abandoned and then waited so long to have back; so much sacrificed for him and seemingly so little to show for it. A life twice disrupted and still not settled. And yet, despite that, here he was standing beside her; sharing something unspoken and profoundly intimate in a room full of people. Words couldn't describe her emotions, but she would not let her voice crack and ruin their gentle harmony.

Later he asked her to sing "I Cried a Tear." She stood alone in the center of the living room holding the mic with both hands. Her voice faltered, but neither of them was embarrassed by it. There was something special happening, something restorative and lasting, something that helped Marcus to solve the dilemmas of his new muddled world.

The old Cavalier rolled slowly through the suburban streets. Marcus's mother hummed lightly and Marcus watched her. "I had a good time with you today, Mama."

His mother smiled at the road. "I love you, *anak*."

Marcus leaned forward, placing his elbows on the seats in front of him. "I love.... I mean, *mahal din kita Nay*." The world was all right.

No Squatters

"Divisoria," he directed the cab driver in Tagalog. "I want to do some Christmas shopping for the family."

The driver smiled. "Yes, sir."

The car turned and accelerated and stopped and started again, winding through the narrow streets. The two men talked casually while Christmas carols played softly from the speakers.

"Maybe you should lock your door, sir," the driver advised. "It's shorter to go through Tondo."

The man did as advised and watched carefully out his window. He had never been to Tondo, but he had heard plenty of stories. None of them good. Thieves and beggars, prostitutes and glue sniffers, rapists and killers all supposedly stalked the streets of this forbidden part of town. He observed the changing scenery and his countenance fell. The concrete buildings of the city abruptly gave way to indistinguishable rows of densely-packed dwellings. The makeshift shacks were patched together with scraps of metal or cardboard or stiff pieces of canvas and held in place with twine and wire. They looked both abandoned and infested and ready to collapse. Despite the diversity of building materials, the landscape reflected only shades ranging from black to charcoal grey. Children of both genders wondered the streets in threadbare tee-shirts and cut-off shorts and nothing to cover their feet. Their thin bodies were stained with dark smudges and odd shaped patches that seemed to be more than dirt. The man remarked how women seemed to vastly outnumbered men. The driver agreed and dared him to find one that wasn't pregnant.

Despair and hopelessness seeped into the cracks and coated the streets. The man gave his door a quick tug to make sure it was fully closed and glanced at the lock. The entire landscape seemed to gasp for air but only inhaled enough to stave off death for another fleeting moment. The man was unsettled. Despite multiple encounters with poverty over the past few years in the Philippines and elsewhere, this one penetrated him deeply and cast doubts in vulnerable spaces in his mind that he struggles with still.

"Why don't they do something?"

"Who?"

The man's eyes darted around as if searching for an answer. "I don't know, they.... the government, the churches, NGOs, the UN for heaven sake."

The driver looked in his rearview mirror. "About what?"

The man nodded sharply at his window. "About this. Why don't they do something about this?"

The driver shook his head and smiled sarcastically. "Oh, this. Yes, well, they do do something about this."

"What?"

The driver lit up a cigarette and blew the smoke out a cracked window. "Well, they've got some programs. The government gives away rice every once and a while. Family planners and nurses come down to check them out sometimes." He coughed and took another drag and blew it in the car this time. "Then there's the religious groups. They preach them the Word and try to rehabilitate the prostitutes and the glue sniffers, but they don't last long. Look around. Who would want to spend much time here?"

The man leaned back and looked at the driver in the mirror. "I don't think it looks all that dangerous, really. Just poor. I would like to help them."

The driver laughed and let off the gas. "Would you like to get out here then?" The man shook his head and the driver chuckled again. "I guess we should be glad it's here, though. They're not good for business on the pier, but it's better than having them squat all over the city."

"Squat?"

"Yes, squat. They'll infest every corner and crevasse in Manila if they let them. Then you can't get rid of them."

The man became agitated and indignant. "Don't you want to help them? How can you drive through this every day and shrug it off?"

The driver smoked the last of his cigarette and flicked it out the window, undisturbed by the subtle condemnation. "Sure, I'd like to help." He grew thoughtful. "But what is helpful isn't always best. Do you know what I mean?"

The man shook his head. "No, I don't know what you mean."

The driver looked out over the streets. "Those with power have their own programs and ways of keeping a lid on things. It's best not to get involved; otherwise *you* might get caught up in one of their programs." He winked in the mirror.

The man remained silent until the cab rolled up beside a long building at Divisoria.

"Here we are, sir. Merry Christmas and you stay safe."

The man gave the driver a one-hundred peso bill for a seventy peso fare, closed the door and then gripped his bag tightly and walked into the market.

❧

Victor sat down to dinner with his Auntie Gina at a little past nine. It was late, but it was it was Christmastime. Schedules meant even less than they normally do so close to the holidays. He splurged on a whole spit-roasted chicken and two two-liter bottles of coke. It was money he should have saved, but Christmas seemed to loosen pocketbooks all over the city, so his guilt quickly passed. Auntie Gina didn't complain either.

Alena came in around 9:15. The meal was already half over, but Victor rose respectfully and offered her a folding metal chair and glass plate, even though it was her own house. The juvenile twenty-year-old joined them without a word and sat picking pieces of meat off a chicken leg and dipping it in a spicy sauce while texting with her other hand. "You know there's a fire outside," she said nonchalantly after several minutes. Victor and Auntie Gina looked up, but Alena's expression was indifferent. Her phone buzzed on the table and she picked it up again, punched buttons and then set it back down.

"Where?"

"Oh, up the street a ways," she said, nibbling at a stubborn piece of meat, still studying her phone.

Victor and Auntie Gina looked at each other and then looked back at Alena. She offered nothing more. Victor shrugged finally and then scooped another spoonful of rice from a steel pot. Everyone ate in silence.

After several minutes someone shouted imperceptibly from the street, cars honked and a mass of flip-flops clapped on the concrete streets. "What do you suppose all that is?" asked Auntie Gina to no one in particular.

Alena shrugged without looking up from her phone. "Maybe it has something to do with the fire."

Victor stood, suddenly alarmed. His chair scraped along the cement floor, almost tipping over. "I'd better check it out," he said, and dropped his fork and spoon with a loud clank and rushed out the door.

The gray alley walls leading to the street were already awash in an ominous orange glow when Victor stepped outside. He held up his hand to analyze the color reflecting back off his russet skin. It was odd and unsettling, like the calm heaviness before a typhoon. Sweat beaded on his forehead and great gulps of blood rushed to his head.

The usually quiet Manila street was already packed with several hundred wide-eyed onlookers when Victor exited the alley. Local residents cautiously emerged from their wooden or concrete dwellings and clutched their children while gazing at the horrifying spectacle only three or four blocks away. Victor joined the gawking crowds and stared along with them. The flames already reached several stories high. They rolled and flickered and lapped at the night sky as if trying to consume the heavens themselves. Black smoke billowed forth, enhancing the range and intensity of the inferno's glow. The noxious cloud hung low above the street and curled over the dilapidated two-story buildings as if scouting potential routes for what followed.

Victor watched the blaze for several minutes, trying to deduce its motives or discover a method to its movement. It was useless. There was none. It felt nothing but hunger. It knew nothing but destruction. It didn't care what Victor observed or how he strategized, it would do as it wished. This realization eventually struck him like a gunshot. Panic rose in his chest as he pushed his way through the crowd back toward the alley, stumbling and scuffing the tip of his flip-flops on the coarse street.

Auntie Gina and Alena sat quietly on a rattan couch scanning three local channels for news. There wasn't any. Victor burst in, wild-eyed and breathing heavily. "We need to make a plan," he said, trying to take the edge off his voice. "The fire is spreading fast. It's already reached the pharmacy." Auntie Gina crossed herself while Alena rose defensively. "I mean just in case," Victor added trying to take back is sense of urgency. Auntie Gina began to cry.

"I want to see it," Alena declared. Her voice had an edge of skepticism.

Victor let out an indignant huff. "I think you better get your most important items gathered up just in case." He reached down and started stacking small cardboard Kodak booklets filled with photographs.

Alena stomped past him and out the door into the alley. Auntie Gina followed. Victor shook his head. By the time the three of them made it back down the concrete corridor, the street was already overflowing with dozens of refugees working against the crowds. They were loaded down with all the clothes, appliances, and children they could carry; metal pots and electric fans, pieces of silverware and crumpled blankets clanked and dragged along the street amidst the garbage and scattered bits of junk left behind. The pitiful people stumbled and lurched and sobbed bitterly as they meandered down the streets to heaven knows where, their hair and clothes singed black and their skin already shimmering with ruddy burns and delicate blisters.

The fire had spread rapidly through a series of wooden shops and then crossed the street about three blocks away. The heat was already intense on Victor's face. He shielded it and then removed his hand to gain a sense of its intensity. Auntie Gina stood motionless with her daughter, their eyes wide with terror. "Auntie, go pack up what's important and get ready to run if we have to," Victor commanded.

She blinked several times and her eyes glistening in the orange glow. "All right," she quietly conceded. Alena followed her back down the alley without argument and set to work organizing and packing her life.

Victor cut through the crowd, his mind craving information for the inevitable decisions he would have to make. He examined the fire again and tried to determine its trajectory. Several fire trucks had arrived from the other direction, but their meager output wasn't making the slightest difference. He looked back up the street toward the alley. More fire trucks lay in the distance but access was difficult, if not impossible. The street overflowed now with thousands of onlookers and refugees, making it impenetrable. Victor cursed them out loud, though he was certainly part of the problem himself. He looked them over again, and then took in a deep breath and shoved his way back through the masses away from the fire.

Near the alley he watched a small barangay official wearing an orange vest and thick glasses desperately trying to clear a path for the fire engines. The man pleaded and reasoned and gently guided people with his hands, but very few complied. He looked lost and confused and unequal to the task, like a poor itinerant preacher warning the world of an impending apocalypse, with none giving heed to his message. Victor cursed him for his inadequacy but immediately felt bad about it. He eventually made his way to a large yellow fire engine marked "Quezon City FD" and climbed the spiky steps, leaning close to the window.

The driver looked surprised. "What the hell do you think you are doing?"

Victor held tightly to the door. "Just lay on your horn and don't let up. Then drive through the crowd. They'll move."

The driver pushed the brim of his hat up. It was much too big for his head and it flopped back farther than he intended. He was already sweating profusely under his coat. He regarded Victor carefully and then looked at the firefighter in the passenger seat for guidance. The man shrugged. He looked back at Victor. "Are you some kind of official?"

Victor searched the crowd briefly for the man in the orange vest but he was lost in the shifting throngs. "No," he admitted.

"I'm not, but I was sent here by one. A barangay official in an orange vest asked me to deliver that message to you. We need to stop the fire before it gets to the market."

The driver took in a deep breath and let it out slowly, and then wiped his brow with a white cloth and pulled the brim of his hat back down. "All right then," he decided finally, "let's go." He trapped Victor's hand against the door before he could step down. "You get out there in front of us and get their attention on the ground. I'm not running over anyone tonight. Do you understand me? I'll blame you if I do." Victor nodded and hopped onto the pavement.

He marched out in front of the truck shouting and pushing the crowd from the streets. The fire engine's horn blasted and its sirens wailed. The sound seemed to penetrate Victor's skull and rattle his bones, but he kept at his task. Terrified onlookers and shocked refugees were shoved and cursed as Victor struggled against the mass of humanity. He didn't look at their faces; he couldn't bear to. They had, or were about to, lose everything in the world, and he was shoving them for their trouble. But what else could they do but look on; stare numbly at the consuming inferno and confirm what they already knew?

Eventually the multitude began to give way. Victor walked ahead until he couldn't stand the heat and then stepped aside. Several trucks passed—Quezon City FD, Manila FD, the Chinese Volunteers from Binondo, and others. They opened their hoses and sent up rainbows of white liquid that hissed and steamed, but ultimately had little effect. The water seemed to evaporate before it even reached the flames. Several blocks down, a half-dozen trucks had managed to douse the genesis of the disaster, more because there was nothing left to burn than because of an excess of water. It didn't matter now anyway. Victor watched the blaze curl around the block to the west. He could see the flames raging behind the buildings across the street from Auntie Gina's. It wouldn't be long now. He looked up and prayed in the direction of the black cloud hovering over him. He searched for something hopeful in the sky: what, he couldn't imagine. But the end he saw nothing save the blackness, and his prayers seemed to choke in the vapors and die.

It took five agonizing minutes to fight against the crowds back to the alley. Victor peered into the gray hollow-block corridor. Clothes and appliances lay in piles against the walls. Exhausted refugees squatted on their heels with their faces buried in their hands. Victor leaned against a wall to catch his breath and regarded the multitude. He eyes rested on a family of five huddled around a small pile of possessions. The mother clutched two small children while the father tried to think things through. The children were crying. The father paced and looked at the fire, and then looked at his family and then back again and he clenched his fists. Finally he took his ten-year-old son by the shoulders and instructed him to watch over their possessions while he tried to find a safer place for the others. His voice was severe and desperate. The boy nodded, tears streaming down his dirty face. When he was convinced the boy understood, the man disappeared with his wife and two children, leaving the child to weep alone. Victor choked out a sob but dug his fingers into the back of his arm to bury it and then walked down the alley past the boy.

"We're going to have to move down the street," he announced as he entered the little house.

Auntie Gina was stacking shoe boxes and photo albums in a metal dog cage with wheels. She didn't look up. Her hands moved awkwardly as she sifted through a lifetime of possessions and shoved them into boxes. Alena stood watching her with a bulging pink backpack slung over her shoulder and a small radio in her right hand. Her youthful arrogance was gone, replaced by concern and fear. Victor searched out her eyes and gave a small comforting smile. She nodded slightly but didn't smile back.

Precious time ticked away. The orange glow outside loomed greater, becoming more sinister with every passing second. Victor glanced at the clock. 11:26 pm. "We better go with what we have. Let's get this out and then I'll come back for more if I can. You both need to be in a safe place." He moved his hand in a circle toward the door as if he were directing traffic.

Auntie Gina stood, silent tears running down her face. "All right," she said in an even voice. "Let's go." She looked around her simple abode, perhaps for the last time, and then walked out into the alley.

Victor grabbed the dog cage and wheeled it out the door behind her. The alley was almost impassable. Some of the piles were abandoned. He lifted the cage and dragged it, twisting it through the mess. As he neared the exit he instinctively searched for the boy he'd seen earlier. The young man lay sprawled out over his family's possessions. Exhausted by his task and the trauma of the event, he couldn't stave off sleep, and it overtook him. His father hadn't returned yet. His arms and legs rested strategically over as many items as possible so he would be aroused if someone tried to remove something. His face looked calm, relaxed in the sublime escape of unconsciousness. Victor felt another sob struggling to get out. This time he couldn't hold it back. His body shook several times and his throat ached around his Adam's apple as he attempted to suppress his emotions, but they bubbled up briefly and he pretended to look back at the apartment to hide it.

After gaining his composure, Victor bent down and shook the boy softly. His eyes opened instantly, wild and afraid. He sat up with his arms outstretched as if to ward off an attacker. "It's all right." Victor spoke in a soft voice. "It's not safe here anymore. You have to come with us." The boy shook his head. Victor looked down the alley and then stood and checked the progress of the fire. It was close. He squatted again. "Look, just come with me now and I'll come back and get your stuff." The boy knit his brow. Victor grew impatient, but stayed calm. "You can come with me and help me carry it." The boy considered Victor's offer for a long while and finally nodded. Then he rose and grabbed an electric fan and a photo album and followed Victor out into the street.

They walked five blocks up the road and stopped and turned around. It was already too late to go back. The flames were lapping at the building across the street from Auntie Gina's. The boy didn't mention Victor's promise or ask to go back. He just stood, his eyes transfixed on the inferno like everyone else. He softly took Victor's hand and touched the back of it to his cheek and then let it go. The crowd remained quiet and still as they watched. The only reaction came when the flames occasionally breached the walls of a propane tank somewhere and sent an earth-shattering boom though the night air. The congregation would all snap to attention and duck slightly in unison, but no one moved from their place. For the next three hours the fire raged, dimmed, and was eventually contained. Victor lost sight of his Auntie's house in the black billowing smoke, and gave up watching all together in the early morning. Then he, like many others around him, faded into an uneasy sleep in the middle of the dirty street.

❧

The crowds were roused and dispersed by police shortly after 5 am to allow traffic to pass through. Thousands of refugees still littered the streets. The cars honked and swerved and raced by, missing some by only inches, but never looking back. The masses sat on their remaining possessions by the side of the road, bleary-eyed and covered in smoke soot, waiting for relief trucks that wouldn't arrive for another nine hours. Victor gazed over the scene. The boy was gone. Auntie Gina and Jona sat silently next to the dog cage. He stood and coughed and wiped his face on his sleeve and then set off down the street.

Two entire city blocks had burned to the ground and three others were significantly damaged. He walked down the alley, running his hand along the blackened walls. Chunks of charred cement crumbled off and fell like ash to the ground. Auntie

Gina's house was still intact but badly damaged. The corrugated tin roofing curled up from the edges and formed weird shapes against the morning sky. Her orchids were little more than dried twigs and the statue of the Virgin Mother looked like a charred effigy. Inside, the house wreaked of melted plastic and burned metal. The table and chairs lay contorted and smooth, like some strange work of modern art. He examined the television and the mattresses and sifted through some items with the bottom of his flip-flop, but there was nothing there. He squatted and shook his head and then walked out without closing the door behind him.

Further down the street he surveyed the charred piles of cinderblock and rebar and watched the remaining columns of gray smoke twist and curl and then disappear in the air. Dozens of men had already begun salvaging any metal items they could sell for scrap. Tin roofing, shattered gas tanks, hollowed-out refrigerators, bedsprings, and bits of silverware were all arranged in jagged piles on the sidewalk. The men worked without shirts and seemingly without consciousness. Their eyes were dead and their movements robotic as they sifted through the rubble.

Victor approached a police officer who was supposed to be directing traffic away from the mess. He stood in his starched blue uniform, leaning against a charred light pole fanning himself with a handkerchief. The vehicles halted and honked and cut each other off to avoid the rubble, and passed without looking at the cop. "What happened here?" Victor asked, though he was obviously a victim.

The policeman looked around and then looked at Victor. "There was a fire."

Victor let out a blast of air. "I know that. How did it start?"

The cop spit on the ground and then lit up a cigarette and threw the smoking match on the sidewalk. "How do you think?" He glared at the men salvaging metal. "It was those damn squatters, of course. They infested every corner of this street, building their houses out of cardboard and wooden scraps and cooking their meals over open fires. It was only a matter of time."

Victor glanced at the men as well and studied their smudged and mournful faces. "Do they know that for sure? I mean did the fire department do an investigation?"

The cop held his cigarette between his fingers like pencil and blew out a cone of white smoke. "No need. We already know what happened. I just told you what happened, it was the squatters." He looked at the toiling men again and said in a loud voice, "Now they'll have to find some other place to ruin."

Victor nodded and turned away, repulsed by the cop's tone. He walked closer to the charred remains and sat on his heels, trying to comprehend the damage around him.

A voice whispered angrily from behind, "It's not true!"

Victor turned and stared. The whispering man was shirtless, his bare torso covered in black smudges and ruby-colored scratches from the metal. His eyes were bloodshot and angry as they flitted to the cop and back to Victor.

"What's not true?" Victor asked, trying to look indifferent.

"We didn't start this fire." Angry tears welled up in the man's eyes. "They did."

"Who?"

"Them." The man nodded at the cop.

Victor shook his head.

"You think I'm lying?"

Victor didn't respond.

"They're going to build a shopping center here. They've been warning us and beating us and tearing our houses down for months." He looked over the blackness. Tears overflowed his eyelids and made bright trails through the soot smudging his cheeks. "They said they'd burn us out if they had to, and now they have."

The cop looked over at Victor and stared for a long while and narrowed his eyes. The man wiped his cheeks and bowed his head and then plodded back to a pile of blackened metal. Victor stared back. A sharp rhythmic tap echoed out over the din of the passing traffic and the scrape of metal on the asphalt. Another man in uniform stood behind the police officer tacking a sigh to the burnt cinderblock. It simply read: "NO SQUATTERS." Victor rose and spat in the ash, and then turned and walked back up the street to Auntie Gina's destroyed apartment.

Filipino Time

David was not what one would call easy-going. Fastidious is the word that probably fitted him best. He was a copy-editor from Sedona, Arizona, and that suited him right down to the ground. The rigid rules of punctuation, the standardization of forms, the symmetry of the words, and the exactness of his craft mirrored his existence perfectly. That is, David's life closely reflected the pages he so meticulously examined. It was regulated, standardized, and easily measured; parceled out into minutes and hours, days and months, but nothing so vague and inclusive as years. There was sleeping time, eating time, recreation time, and, of course, working time, but nothing that exceeded such categories, and certainly nothing that one might call empty time. He was tall and good-looking, but not dashing; clever and quick-witted, but not funny. Much like the works of literature he scanned, his charm was subtle and usually discovered after prolonged exposure.

He met Maria on a cool October evening while attending a reception for a mutual friend. He watched her for a good hour, munching on hors d'oeuvres and sipping from a crystal flute. She chatted and laughed and shook hands with acquaintances and then sat alone for minutes at a time. Her dark gray pantsuit, rectangular-framed glasses and tight ponytail seemed to suggest no nonsense; work-minded perhaps, definitely not looking for a man. He wanted to look away, to forget about her, but he couldn't. The more he studied her, the more compelling she became. He saw something rare inside her; something uninhibited lying just beneath the surface. Not frivolous or cheap like a college party girl, but something uncommonly common, or perhaps folkish. Whatever it was; it was a quality that David had not encountered before. And certainly something he lacked in his own life.

He wiped his damp hands on the back of his Levis and raked his sandy bangs to the side with his fingers and walked over. She smiled warmly. Their conversation was surprisingly effortless. It ran throughout the reception and into the night at an adobe diner selling Tex-Mex cuisine and American hamburgers. She put him at ease, releasing the tension in his jaw and allowing him to slouch for the first time in a long time. She was an immigrant; a Filipina, a gendered rendition of the word he'd never heard before. She came from a province located somewhere in Luzon called Pangasinan. He didn't try repeating it. Her accent was soft and her mannerisms genuine. She was perfection. He knew it that very night. Ten months later they were married.

Their first year of marriage was pure happiness. David worked at his job as usual and Maria found employment as an activities coordinator at a retirement center. David's life remained segmented, but with more categories now. Family time became a prominent fixture. Maria added texture and warmth to his formerly mundane and somewhat sterile life. He listened silent and curious as she talked of the Philippines' exotic wonders. Strange sounding foods, storybook animals, quaint religious practices and quirky cultural traits wove together to form a fantastic land far across the ocean. He shared static-filled phone calls with her parents and siblings, and listened to their broken English and imagined what they were like in person from their voices and photographs. He always told Maria he wanted to see her homeland, but never really foresaw himself going. Seventeen months and four days into their marriage, however, Maria surprised him with two round trip tickets to the Philippines.

"I've been putting money away since the first night we met," she said smiling sweetly. "You're going to know all of me now; who I really am."

David studied the tickets, rotating them one behind the other several times. He smiled at Maria. "This is great but…"

"Don't worry," she assured him. "I already spoke to Jim. He'll give you the time off." She held his face in between her hands. "Everything is taken care of, David." She gazed deeply into his eyes. "I've been waiting a long time for this."

David nodded slowly, rubbing his face against her palms. "All right," he said. "I can't wait."

❧

David stood studying an oversized calendar nailed to a cinderblock wall in the kitchen. The top portion featured a fair-skinned, bikini-clad Filipina staring seductively at the camera. She cradled an auburn bottle of beer in her hands with the words "Red Horse" emblazoned on the label. He ran his finger across the gridded configuration of numbered days. May 18th. Nine of twenty-nine done. Twenty more to go. He pulled the front of his shirt out and flapped it against his chest and wiped his face with his sleeve.

"Good morning sweetheart." Maria wrapped her arms around him from behind and held him close. David balked at her touch, withdrawing slightly from the increased heat it added to his already sticky body. She let go. "What do you want to do today?" There was concern in her voice.

David shrugged.

It wasn't that David was miserable. In fact, he enjoyed the novelty of it all; bucket showers, rattan beds, motorcycles with sidecars, fresh coconuts, new relatives who thought he was great and good-tasting food. In many ways it was just what he thought it would be. And yet, despite these things there was still something off; something disjointed and irregular that left him feeling exposed and out of sorts. He thought it through many times, considering this or that thing, and trying to shrug off his feelings, but they continued to tug at the edges of his mind.

It wasn't really any one thing in particular that bothered him, but rather a lack of something. He missed the structure and direction of his life at home. He missed the categories, the minutes and hours, the scheduled flow of a life spent in pursuit of something. Existence in the Philippines seemed to float weightless somewhere outside of time. Days dragged by without meaning or direction. There was a lot of sitting and talking and eating, and informal social calls to distant relatives and old friends. David listened silently to their native conversations and only spoke when someone offered him the courtesy of an English query. He knew his feelings were silly and out of place on a vacation to his wife's homeland. He chided himself for it. But it was difficult to generate enthusiasm, and Maria grew more concerned.

More than this, however, was what David wouldn't even admit to himself. His time in the Philippines had in some ways become a metaphor for his relationship with Maria. There weren't any problems to speak of. No fights or issues to work through, no lies or secrets. Just a staleness that he never imagined would creep in, but did. The images of the girl he met at the reception, like the fantastic stories of an exotic Philippines had turned out to be an exaggeration, a utopian ideal, a personal indulgence. He kept these disappointments locked away in dark places, but they had a way of intruding, and so silence was his best defense.

"We're planning to go to San Quintin Falls this afternoon," she said, studying his eyes. "You'll love it. It was one of my most favorite places as a child."

David smiled and nodded. The idea did appeal to him. "That sounds nice. What time are we going?"

Maria looked at the ceiling and pursed her lips. "Oh, I don't know. Later sometime. Auntie Jing and Lona are coming over this morning to cook pinekbet for lunch. Then mama will do some laundry." David listened expressionless and Maria watched him carefully. "We'll go," she promised. "Don't worry, you'll have lots of fun."

"Ok," he agreed finally, trying to sound positive. "I'll look forward to it."

Maria nodded and then scanned the kitchen briefly. She snatched up a pile of small gray envelopes with red and blue striped boarders and the words "Air Mail" written across the bottom. She handed them to David. "Why don't you run these to the post office for me this morning? Get out of the house while it's still cool." She smiled encouragingly and kissed him on the lips. "By the time you get back Auntie Jing and Lona will be here. They're going to love you."

David tapped the envelopes into tight order and nodded and then kissed Maria back and turned and walked out the door.

The post office was a broad rectangular building with faded white paint and wide front doors that remained open all the time to let the air in. Its official governmental appearance was accented by a tattered Philippine flag tangled around a tall pole with a brass ball on top and the words "POST OFFICE" hung in tarnished letters over the door. It wasn't far from Maria's house, only three blocks south and two blocks west. David strolled in the sunshine past fruit vendors and shoe repairmen that waved to him and called him "sir." He smiled and nodded at each one but didn't break his gait. The air hung heavy and he sweated profusely.

He stopped in front of the building and looked it over, and then climbed the cement steps to the open doors and peered inside. It was coarse and old-fashioned inside, and smelled of mildew. He surveyed the row of dark wooden square booths set off by iron grates. There were eight in all, but only two were attended by postal employees. There was an old table for writing on, but no pens, and a small shop selling postal supplies. The place was bustling. He watched the patrons holding tightly to their wallets and address books as they sloshed back and forth from one end of the building to the other; buying envelopes and supplies at one end and then addressing them and pasting them shut on the table at the other end. The mahogany floors creaked and voices echoed off the stark concrete walls. The only place not inhabited was a space near the unmanned booths where shafts of white sunlight penetrated through a high window and illuminated bleached rectangles on the floor.

David entered quietly and picked a stall and stood among the waiting crowds. He kept expecting a line to form but none did. Instead the patrons just huddled around the booths in half-circles jockeying for positions near the postal agent. David soon found himself surrounded on all sides, touching other bodies and feeling the damp heat. Still wanting to maintain even the slightest amount of personal space, he left a gap between himself and the person directly in front of him. This lapse in personal fortitude allowed several people all the opportunity they needed to push ahead and slap their mail on the counter before the others. David watched the postal worker and cleared his throat and waited, but she seemed indifferent to the intense competition playing out before her and simply took whatever mail was placed closest on the counter. He thought she might call for order, but she never did.

David sighed and squinted and crumpled his face, but he was the only one. The dozens of other expressions in the crowd didn't seem to show the least bit of angst. In fact, most looked serene. He shook his head in bewilderment. Suddenly music began to play from somewhere behind the metal grates. David ducked and leaned and peered beyond the postal workers into the back. He was surprised, but not surprised, to see several other employees on their feet moving their bodies in synchronized dance to Bayani Agbayani's hit, "*Otso Otso*." He looked at the crowd around him and then back at the dancers. Their shoulders bobbed and their backs arched as they sang along with the chorus, "*Otso otso O! Otso otso O! Otso otso O! Otso otso O! Otso otso na!*" He smiled and shook his head again and chuckled softly as if disbelieving the reality of his circumstances as he looked back at the crowds.

"Do you like Bayani Agbayani?" An elderly woman with gray hair and no teeth tugged at his forearm. She nodded at the workers. "The music, it's a song by Bayani Agbayani. He's also a comedian, you know."

David shook his head.

The woman smiled. "Well, I'm already old, but still know how to do the *Otso Otso*." She let out a raspy giggle but offered no demonstration.

David regarded her curiously. "You speak excellent English," he said.

The old woman nodded in agreement. "I studied in American schools when I was young. I still love to watch American movies. I even understand the new dialects; even the Negroes."

David shuttered at the reference, but she meant no harm by it. "That's very impressive. I would have thought you might have lived in the States for a while."

The woman blushed. "Oh no, not me. They'd never let me in. No land. No bank accounts. I wouldn't even get an interview." She brushed her gray hairs back from her face and smacked her gums. "What are you doing here in Pangasinan anyway?" she asked.

David told her about Maria in a matter-of-fact way, and about her family and explained it was his first time to the Philippines.

The woman listened carefully, nodding at appropriate times and analyzing his statements. "How interesting." She tugged on his arm again. "Tell me your love story."

David knit his brow. "What?"

"Your love story."

David shook his head. The music stopped when the song was over.

The old woman clucked her tongue. "You know, your love story. I know Maria's family, but I didn't know of her wedding. What is your love story?"

David shifted uncomfortably. Several others in the crowd who had been eavesdropping looked at him expectantly. He opened his mouth and hesitated and then let out a gust of exasperated air. "I don't know," he said finally. "It's not really a story. We just met and dated and fell in love and got married, like a million other people. I don't know that I can really tell anything interesting."

The old woman and now at least a half dozen others shook their heads skeptically. A plump woman with cropped hair a few feet away spoke up. "It's always interesting," she declared. "Otherwise you wouldn't have gotten married."

David stared at her, unable to counter her logic. He furrowed his brow and looked at the ceiling and then looked at the floor. He could feel their eyes on him. "All right," he conceded finally. "Well we met at a reception."

"A wedding reception?" someone asked.

David nodded. "Yes. It was for a mutual friend, but we didn't know each other at the time." He chuckled to himself. "I remember I watched her for a long time before I spoke to her."

A few women giggled. "Was she sexy?" Laughter. A man in the back shouted, "Of course she was sexy, she is Filipina!" More laughter.

David laughed as well and let his smile remain for a few extra seconds. "Yes, she was sexy." He looked up thoughtfully. "She was the most beautiful thing I had ever seen." He stopped. Felt silly. Felt corny. Gazed over the faces uncomfortably and shrugged. "And the rest is history."

Most of the patrons in his half-circle were staring at him now, determined not to let him go. Questions shot from all around to keep his story from ending. "What was she wearing?" "When did you say you loved her?" "Did she want to have kids right away?" Others offered queries in Tagalog or Ilokano and were laughed at for doing so.

David held his hands up. "Maybe some other time." Some voiced their opposition. He made a face and then looked around at his surroundings. "We're in a post office. This is a place of business. People need to get their letters mailed. We're taking up space."

He looked with exasperation on those looking back at him. Suddenly no one seemed intent on getting their letters mailed. Some were buying and pasting envelopes, others were handing their items to the postal worker, but no one looked inconvenienced. Even the postal worker performed her tasks while keeping her eyes fixed on David. She smiled encouragingly. The old woman took him by the crook of the arm again and tugged gently. "Don't be in such a hurry. We just met you. Why don't you tell us your story?" Others nodded and voiced encouraging words.

David formed his hand into a C shape and cupped it around his forehead. Then he wiped the sweat off his upper lip with his shirtsleeve. He opened his mouth again, but didn't know where to start. The old woman took his hand and held it softly and eventually he began to speak. The details were random and awkward at first, chaotic in his mind and in his speech. The memories bled together and shifted around. The sequence or the details were off. He transfixed on a point above their heads and stared at it for long periods, looking no one in the face, even though they looked directly at him.

Soon, however, the words began to take over. He spoke of Maria in ways he hadn't since their first months together; with tenderness and fondness. He recalled things he had forgotten and shared details of their emotional intimacy that he hadn't considered for a long time. He related funny stories and tales of his awkward but endearing courtship. Fancy dinners. Christmases. Quiet moments in their little apartment. He was surprised by his own openness. Somewhere in the middle of it all Maria once again became perfection. He contemplated as he talked why such a girl would ever have him, and even asked the question out loud later on. It seemed he was falling in love with her again, with all the intensity and giddiness he had once felt. The listeners laughed and "awed," and some even cried at his love story. And he was astonished.

David strolled out of the post office nearly an hour and fifty-six minutes after he had walked in. He passed the same vendors and shoe repairmen as before, but this time he nodded at them and smiled and studied their faces, examining the lines and expressions. He tried to guess at their stories. He took notice of the smells and colors and watched the great green palm leaves swaying in the breeze. But mostly he thought about his love story.

David found Maria in the kitchen hunched over a white cutting board chopping carrots when he returned. He pulled her around and clutched her close to his body, taking note of the pressure and breathing in her smell. She contorted, trying to keep the knife in her hand away from David, but she didn't resist his embrace. He held her for a while and then kissed up her neck and across her cheek and landed at her lips. She looked at Auntie Jing and her mother. Both were mortified by the open display of affection, but shrugged it off as something peculiarly American. Lona smiled scandalously. But still Maria didn't resist. She set the knife aside and embraced him back and kissed his lips.

"Where have you been?" she asked with slight concern.

He smiled softly and ran his thumb down her cheek. "I've just been passing the time," he said. And then he kissed her again.

A Reckoning

Black clouds rolled in from the west over the sea. Ansar watched as the crystal blue waters turned the color of spilt ink and churned into whitecaps. This was a foreboding sign. He knew they were coming. He knew the direction. "When" was the only lingering question, but certainly the most critical. He squinted against the misty haze that always precedes a downpour during the rainy season. Nothing. He looked back toward the village. Silence.

He pulled up his collar and staked out a spot under a broad banyan tree and stood studying the ocean, straining to detect even the slightest change. The waves splashed and sprayed against the rocks. The seas looked rough. Maybe they turned back. Maybe the messenger from the village down the coast had overreacted.

And then he saw them, moving swiftly through the dark waters to the south. Ansar felt his stomach contort and a tingling sensation rippled through his torso. He pulled a small pair of binoculars from the front pocket of his camouflage jacket. The lenses fogged and he wiped them clean. Two small boats, each containing three or four heavily armed men, their cumbersome rifles the color of the dark waters. There was no mistaking their identity, the worn jungle camo, the checkered head-scarves, and large caliber weapons.

"Damn you," he hissed and put the binoculars back in his front pocket. He looked out across the water and then turned toward the village and looked back again at the boats, suddenly unsure of his next move. He dithered a moment longer and then finally set off toward the village. The dirt road he traveled led directly back into the center of town and eventually up to the mayor's house. Ansar knew the old man was there, waiting for some news, but he decided instead to cut down a small trail heading east to a small cluster of wooden houses set on stilts.

"Father," he called in a desperate shouted whisper. "They're coming."

An aged man with a thin wiry beard and twisted head wrap appeared in the doorway of one of the bamboo dwellings. He looked at Ansar for a long while and Ansar looked back without speaking. The man touched his head wrap and put his forefinger to his lips. "Why do they do this? Are we not fellow Muslims?" Ansar felt tears welling up. He blinked hard, squeezing the obnoxious liquid evenly and imperceptibly across his eyelids to mix with the mist.

After several seconds the man nodded as if coming to agreement with an invisible companion. "Get your mother and sisters and take them to the cota. I'll go inform the mayor."

Ansar hesitated. The man grew impatient and stern. His almond eyes narrowed. "Do exactly as I tell you, boy. Do you understand? Listen to your father." Ansar felt the tears gather again, but rushed to an adjacent stilted house before his father could detect his emotion.

"Let's go," he announced. "Father said to hike up to the cota." A slender woman in a black hijab nodded, anticipating his instructions before he let them out, and grabbed two little girls by the hand. The four of them hiked single file up a narrow trail cut through suffocatingly dense foliage. The woman led the way while Ansar lingered in the rear. It wasn't far, but it was arduous.

It took just over twenty minutes to ascend the hillside. The cota was an old earthen structure dating back to the American period. Nineteen thirties maybe. It had been rebuilt many times but was in a dilapidated state when they arrived. Ansar pushed open the wooden door and stepped inside ahead of his mother. Not much to see but four mud brick walls and some crumbled quarters sprouting saplings and emerald green vines. The woman led her girls to a row of pulverized earth and sat them down and wiped the sweat from their eyes. They were frightened, but thankfully could not fully comprehend the weight of their circumstances. Ansar lingered at the door, and then opened it and stepped outside. He looked toward the village. They must be getting close now. He strained to hear something, boat motors, voices—anything—but it was no use. He was much too far away.

"Ansar, come in here, son." The woman stood with her head protruding out from behind the door. "Your father will come get us when it's time."

Ansar didn't move. He took in a deep breath and let it out slowly. "I'm going back down, mama."

The woman stepped out from behind the door and adjusted her hijab. "No you're not. You're staying right here until your father comes to get us."

Ansar kept his head pointed toward the village, consciously avoiding his mother's eyes. "They might need me."

His mother took a step closer. "I said get in the cota, Ansar."

He shook his head and struck an argumentative tone. "I'm seventeen now, mama. The Prophet was leading caravans through bandit-infested deserts at my age."

His mother's eyes grew angry at the comparison. Her voice was low and reverent. "The Prophet's parents were dead when he was your age, Ansar. Now get in the cota."

He sighed deeply and took a step toward his mother. Her expression relaxed. "No," he said, his voice quivering and unsure.

Her eyes widened in shock. "Ansar…"

Without another word the boy turned and ran into the forest before his defiance could fully sink in. "I'm so sorry mama," he whispered, trying to forget the look on her face as he turned his back on her. "They'll be all right," he repeated to himself. "They'll be all right in the cota."

The raindrops fell heavily, soaking though his jacket and turning the trail to mud. His sandals shifted and slid as he tried to stay on the long grass just to the side of the path. After several minutes he arrived outside the village, where he carefully skirted around a cluster of concrete houses and eventually settled into a clump of banana trees beyond the plaza.

His father and the mayor stood under umbrellas muttering to each other in concerned voices. Suddenly they stopped and turned together toward the road heading south out of town. Ansar followed their gaze. Seven men strode slowly through the mist, their rifles swaying in time with their gait. They stopped several yards in front of Ansar's father and the mayor where each group stared speechless at each other for several seconds. Finally a young-looking rebel with a bright red-checkered headscarf and black sub-machine gun spoke.

"Salam," he said, his face turning friendly. "Thank you for coming to greet us in the rain, brothers." No one responded. He smiled and looked at his companions. "Don't worry about us. We're just here to rest." Ansar strained to hear. The broad banana leaves quivered and bounced around him in the pattering rain.

The mayor stepped forward. He was a thin, soft-spoken man of more than sixty years with a patchy beard and a large brown mole above his left eye. His gentle demeanor made him perfectly ill-suited for this type of confrontation. "Yes, of course," he exclaimed in a conciliatory voice. "We'd be happy to get you something to eat and a place out of the rain."

The rebel's eye's narrowed and his grin turned sinister. It was becoming clear that the mayor would be an easy push. "Excellent," he said. "We'll also need some money and young men for the cause."

The mayor stopped and turned slightly. His eyes darted to his companion and then to the rebel's boots as he settled on a response. "Well, we have a bit of money left from zakat that you could have, but," he measured his words carefully, "our young men have gone to Zamboanga looking for work. There's no one here much older than fifteen, and none of them have any military training." His eyes flitted again to Ansar's father for a split second.

The rebel pulled a cigarette and a wooden match from a plastic wrapper in his front pocket. He dried the side of his gun with his sleeve and lit the match and held it to the cigarette. "Well," he said in a thoughtful voice, "why don't you gather everyone together and we'll see what we've got?"

Ansar remained motionless among the green leaves, trying to bury the terror rising in his chest. "This is why you listen to your father," he thought.

The mayor hesitated, desperately searching for an excuse, or at least a way to stall. He stepped closer to the rebel, his eyes pleading and his hands facing upward in supplication. "I don't think there's anyone here you would want. We're just simple Muslims with very little to offer." He invited them on with a downward motion and smiled. "Come, let me get you something to eat. I'll take care of you."

The men stood fast. The lead rebel took a long drag on his cigarette and blew out the smoke in the form of a sigh. "I'm getting tired of this, old man." He wiped water off the submachine gun again and gripped the handle. "Why are you resisting the cause? You are the mayor of a Muslim community. The people should look to you for leadership and example." He pointed the gun barrel accusingly at the old man. "Unless you're a collaborator." The rebel took another thoughtful drag. "That's it, isn't it? You're a collaborator. I can see it clearly now. You probably give those bastards in the Philippine Army more cooperation than you do your own people. They murder and rape Muslims and you get a fancy title. That's it, isn't it?"

The mayor shook his head frantically. "I am a good Muslim," he repeated touching his chest with his forefinger. "I am a good Muslim."

The rebel approached and struck the old man open handed. The mayor stumbled and then collapsed in the mud. He tried to rise, but his hands slipped and he splashed back to the ground. The rebels chuckled and shook their heads.

"Now do as I say and gather the people," he ordered one more time.

The mayor rose to one knee and wiped his hands on his shirt. "Yes, brother. Yes, brother."

Ansar looked around the village. He knew of at least a dozen young men they could press into service. He considered trying to quietly warn those he could, but his tracks and the noisy squish of the mud would inevitably lead to his own capture. He canvassed the village again.

Caught up in these thoughts, Ansar was suddenly startled by a defiant voice. It startled the others as well. "No!" The word hung in the air and echoed over the plaza. Ansar recognized it at once and felt the air leave his lungs. His father strode towards the rebels, his body erect and defiant. "We're not gathering anybody for you to take."

The lead rebel was taken aback momentarily by the man's boldness. His cigarette hung limply out the corner of his mouth as he analyzed Ansar's father. "Who the hell are you?" he asked, regaining his composure.

The old Muslim stood close enough to strike. "I am Hajji Nasar Abdullah Fatani, a proud Tausug and a pious Muslim."

The rebel removed his cigarette and spit in the mud. "That's a long name for someone so worthless to the cause." He clenched the cigarette between his teeth again and sucked in and blew smoke out his nose. Then he chuckled and shook his head. "You can't fool me," he stated flatly. "You're just another collaborator like that old son-of-a-bitch kneeling in the mud." He kicked a spray of brown water at the mayor. Then he turned his back on Ansar's father. "Now do what we ask or we'll kill every one of you, Muslim or not."

Ansar sat silently, begging his father to turn and walk away. Most of the village's young men would surely be in hiding by now. There was no more point to his defiance. He had stalled sufficiently. But the man did not move from his position.

"No," he said again, raising his chin in contempt.

The rebel turned sharply. "What did you say?"

"I said no. You are not a Muslim. We are not obliged to help you."

"Not a Muslim," repeated the rebel thoughtfully.

"That's right. You are nothing but a pirate and a terrorist, killing and robbing your own people in the name of God. May Allah curse you to hell for your bad deeds."

The rebel blinked several times and then let out a short blast of air like a single chuckle at a witty remark. His companions watched him in silence.

Ansar suddenly heard a number of simultaneous but distinct sounds. Two cracks followed close together, like enormous firecrackers during a New Year's celebration in the plaza, but sharper, more violent and menacing. The other sounds were softer, like someone punching a feather pillow with each fist in quick succession, but somehow nauseating. Ansar felt his strength leave him as the shells exploded out of his father back, leaving jagged irregular red holes in his white shirt. The old Muslim wobbled on his feet and then slumped over, falling still into the mud.

Ansar collapsed as well. He lay on his back looking at the banana leaves bouncing in the rain above him. The cold drops pooled around his eyes and ran in streams down his forehead along his hat band. He struggled to comprehend what he just witnessed; what it meant and what it required. His mind moved in strange directions; shock, numbness, and then, somehow, more alert. He became oddly aware of sounds and colors and of his own body. The rebel's voices became more audible.

"Kill the old man and loot the village." Another crack and the sound of another body splashing down in the mud. Ansar rose to his knees and peered through the leaves at the rebels. They had already started to disperse. His mind raced. He surveyed the houses around the plaza, making a systematic inventory. He shook his head and then rubbed his eyes and wiped the water from his face. Then it occurred to him: Uncle Samir's house.

He crept silently along the plaza's eastern edge toward a gray hollow-block structure with a red door and corrugated tin roofing. Most of the rebels gravitated to the mayor's house, but a few lingered back to keep watch.

Ansar paused for only a second to confirm what he had seen. His father lay face down in the mud, his shirt soaked red with blood. No movement. No breath. Silent as a stone. Despite his revulsion and grief, the sight steeled his nerves.

He tiptoed around to the back of his uncle's house, opened the door and stepped inside. He walked slowly, whispering familiar names. Silence. He passed from room to room until he happened upon an old wooden footlocker stamped "US Army" in white stenciled letters. He lifted the latch and raised the lid and began to rifle through its contents. He dug through old clothes, brass betel nut boxes, and wooden knick-knacks. He found the bottom of the locker and ran his hand the width of its base. He paused. There it was, cool and heavy he wrapped his fingers around the barrel of a gun. He lifted it up, cutting though the other items and pulled it out and laid it across his lap. It was an ancient .30 caliber P14 Enfield left by the Americans many years ago. Ansar pulled back the bolt and looked inside. It was empty. He set it aside and began frantically tossing clothes onto the floor. Outside he heard the rebels hoot and laugh. A woman screamed. Ansar refused to consider who and continued searching. He ran his hand along the bottom edges, again searching the corners and squeezing bundles of cloth. His thumb encountered something sharp. He lifted the magazine and inspected it. Six shells. He shoved it in the gun and the action snapped. He looked around one more time. Clothes and personal items were strewn about the floor. His eyes rested momentarily on a large brass box, too big for betel nut. He knelt and lifted the lid. Inside was a tarnished semi-automatic Colt .45. He ejected the magazine. Seven shells. The firing chamber was empty. He counted in his mind. Thirteen shots. But how many rebels? He closed his eyes and thought back, but only images of his father appeared, and his eyes shot open again. "Can't be more than thirteen," he thought, although he knew the odds of each bullet finding a target were impossibly low.

He crept to a front window and peered out. The plaza was obscured by several small houses and a big banyan tree. He could hear voices, though. Four of them maybe. He could also hear the woman crying. He slung the leather strap over his shoulder and let the rifle rest between his shoulder blades. He then shoved the .45 in his pants and crept out the back door.

He considered carefully what lay ahead. Taking a life. There was plenty of that going on in Mindanao and Sulu. Murders and massacres were not uncommon occurrences, but Ansar had never actually been part of such things. He had only witnessed their aftermath, the tears and the wails, the devastated families and escalating feuds. He was a part of one now, though. He was going to kill a man; several if he got the chance. He let this sink in. It wasn't pleasant like he expected. There was no lust for blood or white-hot rage clouding his thoughts. It was just a simple but unavoidable feeling of obligation. There had to be a reckoning for his father's death. Emotions would catch up and take their toll later. They would only be a liability now.

He walked low and slow around the plaza, trying to keep his hands and the guns clean and dry. He halted and looked out over the town. He could see three rebels standing in a circle smoking cigarettes over a burgeoning pile of loot at their feet. Sacks of rice, family heirlooms, and a few outdated firearms lay on a canvas tarp. The rain began to let up. Ansar watched closely for movement in the houses. He saw dark figures appear in windows across the way and heard the uneven clanks and scrapes of rummaging. It became increasingly and frustratingly impossible to determine or recall their exact number. He needed to get a better vantage point. Somewhere higher. He studied the village's shapes and nooks. Trees were no good in the rain. And even if it were dry there would be no escaping from a tree once shots were fired. Not that Ansar was afraid to die this day. In fact, he fully expected it. But he wouldn't waste his opportunity sitting precariously in a tree.

The highest stable point in town was the minaret. It wasn't a big mosque. Maybe a thousand square feet. But the minaret stood a good 30 feet off the ground. It didn't provide a lot of cover if they returned fire, but he could duck down the narrow spiral staircase, perhaps before they even knew where the shots originated. He thought it through several times, imagining various scenarios and playing out events in his mind. In the end, the minaret seemed to be better than the other alternatives and so he settled on the idea.

He wound his way toward the mosque, pausing occasionally to check the rebels and scan for movement. The town was eerily silent except for the muffled sounds of looting. Most residents had surely evacuated after hearing the shots. He wondered about his mother and sisters. The refugees would have left an obvious trail to the cota. He thought about this carefully for a moment. He simply had to kill as many as possible, that was all there was to it.

Ansar pushed open the heavy door at the back of the mosque. He half expected to find groups of shivering villagers seeking refuge inside, but it was empty. No man could abandon his kin and no woman would pollute the holy place. He was relieved by the solitude.

He walked respectfully over the cement floor and sidestepped a prayer rug, feeling guilty for carrying instruments of destruction through a house of God. He removed the rifle strap and held the gun with both hands while ascending a spiraled metal staircase to the top of the minaret. He crouched and scooted through the small arched opening onto a narrow circular balcony and sat for several seconds behind the wall. After summoning as much courage as possible, he removed his hat and peeked over the edge. The cover wasn't as good as he originally thought. He'd be easy to spot, especially with a rifle hanging out. He would just have to watch and wait and act quickly when the opportunity arrived.

The rebels, now four in number, stood in the same circle around the growing pile of loot. Ansar continued peeking every ten to twenty seconds, raising his eyes slightly above the circular railing. It was hot. The steamy air and the anxiety of his predicament produced droplets of sweat that saturated his clothes and stung his eyes. Time passed. Ansar inspected his weapons trying to get a feel for their weight and nuances. It was impossible to tell how they would perform. He wiped his eyes roughly with the heels of his hands and peered over the railing again. The circle had grown to six. Two were squatted down sorting through the materials. Two stood in conversation, smoking and spitting in the mud. Another two stood idly by, resting their arms on their guns. The rebel leader was still not among them.

His father's body lay in the mud not far away. The rebels took no notice of it. Ansar struggled to ignore it as well, but it was the first and last thing he saw every time he peeked over the railing. He tried not to comprehend his circumstances—what happened, what will happen. He felt the tears and grief welling up in places deep inside. He gripped the gun tighter and tried to think strategically but his thoughts were fuzzy and punctuated with pain. He played out various scenarios again and again to shout down his emotions.

Six shells in his rifle. It wouldn't be enough. He cursed the old gun quietly and immediately repented. Finally, he determined to shoot when the rebel leader arrived and kill as many as possible before they scattered and hunted him down and killed him too. It was the best he could hope for. He could not turn back or reconsider now. There was always the .45, but it would be useless from the minaret, especially once they determined his position and opened up with automatic weapons.

More time passed. His legs cramped as his cells dehydrated. He glanced over the railing again. Seven now. The rebel leader stood slightly separated from the group studying a laminated map. The size of the group seemed similar to what he had seen earlier. There was no way to be sure. One or two more could be lingering elsewhere, but probably not. Ansar quietly raised the rifle and rested it on the railing. He would be easy to spot now. Time was short. He cocked the weapon and trained the sights on the rebel leader. He felt sick to his stomach. It churned and jumped as his body rebelled against his mind. He took a deep breath and held it and squeezed the trigger twice in quick succession. Crack. Crack. The bullets whizzed down, the first imbedding itself in the back of the rebel leader's left arm, the other splashing into the mud just beyond him. The world seemed surreal once it began. Ansar pivoted the rifle slightly on the railing toward the cluster of rebels. They stood frozen, disoriented, looking around wildly for the shooter. Ansar pulled the trigger four more times. The explosions seemed distant and muffled. The shells hissed and ripped through various parts of the rebels' bodies; a neck, a torso, the small of one's back, just below the collarbone of another. Four rebels wilted into the mud, one of them dead, another not far behind. The other two screamed in shock and agony and writhed in the soupy mess.

Ansar dropped the Enfield over the railing and crouched down low. His chest tightened and seized in a series of sobs. The shots, the impact, the tearing of flesh, the blood, the screams all overwhelmed him. He vomited and wiped his mouth with his sleeve and heaved again.

It took only seconds for the rebels to determine his position. Dozens of projectiles whined and clapped against the minaret, sending up small clouds of cement dust. Ansar held his breath to quiet the sobs and jerked the .45 from his belt. Only one rifle continued firing after the initial burst. Ansar heard the rebel leader cursing and barking orders to get the wounded to the boats.

"How many shooters?" shouted a desperate voice.

"I don't know. Just one I think. Get them to the boats."

The desperate voice shook unevenly. "Bashir and Karam are dead."

A man screamed in pain. More panicked voices. "Rasul is bleeding badly. I think it's his liver."

The rebel leader cursed louder and shot four more times at the minaret. "Damn it! Fine, pick him up and get the hell out of here." He paused. "Bakri, you get the sacks of rice and anything that's small and valuable."

Barkri mentioned something about the leader's bloody arm.

"Just do as you're told or I'll shoot you myself. I'm not leaving 'til I kill that son-of-a-bitch. Now give me the machine pistol and get to the boats."

The rebels splashed through the mud carrying their comrades as Ansar descended the spiral staircase pointing the gun out before him. He wasn't ready to die yet, but he wasn't entirely ready to kill again either. He just wanted to survive, to get to his mother and sisters, to grieve for his father. He stopped at the bottom of the staircase and listened and surveyed the doors and windows. Nothing. His body quivered and his breathing was shallow. He watched the wooden door. There were footsteps in the mud. They clapped a couple times on the cement porch and stopped. Ansar crouched a little lower. Suddenly the machine pistol rattled and the door jerked open in a cloud of splinters and dust. The bullets zipped and embedded themselves into the wall just to the left of where the imam stood to lead prayers. Ansar jumped at the commotion and inadvertently fired a shot, where he couldn't guess. He found his nerves and slipped into a small space beneath the minbar. It was wooden and wouldn't hold up against bullets, but it was cover.

The rebel walked slowly through the mosque, his left arm dangling. Streams of blood streaked down his hand and dripped heavy drops from all four of his fingers. He was silent except for his steps. He paused in the middle of the Mosque and looked around as if he had never been in such a place. He studied the walls and the ceiling, the prayer rug and the minbar. He lifted the gun and walked toward the spiraled staircase. Ansar followed him with his ears, counting the steps and determining his distance. The rebel stopped, bent over and looked up the twisted steps. Ansar emerged silently from the minbar and stood facing the rebel's back. He raised the .45 and leveled it, aiming in between his target's shoulder blades. He then closed his eyes and pulled the trigger five times in quick succession. The shots cracked and echoed off the mosque walls, sharp metallic high-pitched sounds that rang out at odd angles. The first three bullets tore through the rebel's torso forming an uneven left to right pattern, the last entering just above his should blade and exiting under his collarbone. The other two buzzed off, hitting a wall and smashing through a glass window.

Ansar kept his eyes closed for several seconds longer. The rebel fell awkwardly on his side with the machine pistol still in his grip. He gurgled and spit bloody, imperceptible cursings and tried to raise his weapon, but his arm was useless. Ansar opened his eyes and stared at the damage he inflicted through the blue smoky haze. He shook and sobbed like a child lost in the market. This was not what his father would have wanted. This is not what he wanted either, but here he was. He walked up to the bullet-ridden body and gazed into the rebel's wild eyes, angry and insane, slowly losing touch with reality and consciousness, unable to comprehend the devastating affliction that incapacitated him. Ansar raised the .45 again and a shot rang out. Blood pooled on the mosque floor.

The Call

Rolando watched his daughter sleeping soundly on a rattan bed. She still wore her school uniform. The blue pleated skirt wound tightly around her legs and gathered into an awkward lump under her knees where she'd rolled and twisted it around her. Her white blouse lay wrinkled and stretched over her thin torso, her necktie tossed haphazardly on the floor. She rested peacefully despite her disheveled appearance, and breathed evenly in the cool night air.

Rolando checked the clock on his cell phone and stood and paced over the gritty cement floor in his bare feet. Then he sat, and illuminated the phone again by pushing a button. It was already past ten o'clock. She should have called by now. She said she would call at ten. He shook his head and exhaled through tight lips. Sometime he wondered if she had forgotten all about them; if he and the little girl had somewhere along the line faded into bland strokes, like impressionist paintings that depicted bygone eras.

She had been gone now for two years, seven months, and twelve days. He closed his eyes, leaned his head on his fist and thought of her departure, as he often did. It was his last memory of her, raw and looming, imminent at the edges of his mind and prone to intrude at inconvenient times. He stood on the other side of a fenced barrier holding his daughter's hand and sobbing in front of the shuffling crowds. He followed his wife along the railing as the line moved, telling her he loved her and kissing her and lifting his daughter for embraces over the railing, and then setting the child down and kissing his wife again and wiping his nose with the back of his hand. She said she loved them too, but shed no tears. He told her she didn't have to go; that it would be all right, that he would find a way, that it was his job to take care of the family and he would do it. She shook her head and reminded him of the debts they had already acquired just to buy the open ticket to Hong Kong. She spoke coldly of their daughter's prospects for a prosperous life without capital, without backing, without a mother working abroad. He shook his head again and warned her of abuses and plots and misdeeds and corrupt employers, and things he had read in the papers and seen on late night television newscasts, and begged her again to stay for her own sake. She touched his lips and held his head to her breast like a child. She stroked his hair and told him not to worry. And so he stood quietly sobbing with the child until she passed through the electric sliding doors and out of their lives.

The eleven-year-old girl stirred and scratched her neck and swept her hair back from her face without waking. Rolando rose and fanned her with a Hello Kitty folder he took from her backpack. The child's math homework slid out halfway and he pushed it back in and sat down. He knew his wife wouldn't approve of their daughter sleeping in her school uniform, but then again she didn't approve of a lot of Rolando's decisions around the house, and so he simply wouldn't mention it to her, like so many other passing details they used to share. He stared dully into the blackness and waited with the cell phone still in his hand.

Mae sat silently on the corner of her bed, listening. She could make out the measured sound of breathing through the thin, asylum-like apartment walls. The child slept and she thanked the saints. He was a light sleeper and a tremendous crier, and Mae was often forced to lay with him until he returned to sleep. She spent many such nights contorted awkwardly, cramping, but afraid to move lest the child woke and irritate her employers. And thus she passed her hours, both day and night, next to this child that was not her own; feeding it, bathing it, speaking softly and cooing to it in broken Cantonese. She heeded the child's every whim, but she cared nothing for it. It was not hers. She missed her daughter and sang Tagalog songs to the Chinese baby and recited nursery rhymes to it in foreign tongues, and cried and hid her face when the child looked at her.

All was silent. Mae lifted the receiver of a thin white telephone with oversized black buttons and dialed an extended series of numbers on the back of a tattered calling card. The phone rang twice and Rolando picked up.

"Hello?"

"Hello."

She put the receiver against her shoulder and listened carefully.

"Mae, is that you? Hello? Hello?"

She put the receiver back against her ear. "Yes, it's me. I have to make sure the child is sleeping. If he wakes I'll have to go." She listened again and Rolando waited. Finally she came back on.

"Are you there?" he asked.

"Yes, I'm here."

"Oh. Well, how are you?" The question sounded formal and inane, but what else could he ask? And so he waited patiently for a response.

"I'm fine. How are you?"

"I'm fine too." He shifted in his seat and closed his eyes and gave his head a quick shake. "I mean, we're doing well. I'm glad you called. I was waiting for your call. I wish you could call while Christina is still awake. It's been almost a week."

Mae bit her lower lip and exhaled into the phone. "Please don't do that. You know how strict they are."

Rolando nodded with the phone. "I know. Sorry."

"So how is our little girl?"

Roland repeated the word, "little," and imagined what it meant to his wife so far away. He told her of Christina's schooling, and of her grades, and of various projects and accomplishments she had achieved, and how she was growing, and what size her shoes were, and how long her hair had gotten and how she wore it. Mae listened silently to every word but offered no questions or comments. What could she say? He spoke of a girl she didn't know; a phantom that always floated just beyond the senses, but one that she feared terribly.

He spoke on and on, rambled and stopped and then spoke again, wishing his wife would ask particular questions, but she didn't. Finally he drew a deep breath and attempted a foray into murky waters. "Mae, I need to tell you something else about Christina."

Mae pressed the phone close to her ear. "All right," she encouraged. "What is it?"

Rolando fumbled with the phone and switched it to the other ear and then withdrew it and coughed and put it back. "Well, um… she … uh. It's like this, really. Last week I got a text from a teacher at her school and…"

"Can you hold on a minute?"

"Sure."

The phone tapped and scraped through the line as Mae put the receiver down on the table. She laid her ear against the wall and listened. The child stirred and whined thinly and knocked against the wall once. Mae kept her hear to the wall, breathing in shallow, silent breaths.

Rolando listened to the silence and tried to frame his subject for when she came back on, but there were no words. How could he tell it? How could he tell of the panic and embarrassment; his attempts to be nurturing and his ultimate failure as a parent? How could he tell of the text that simply read: "Medcl emrgncy pls come?" How could he describe the disheveled, sobbing young girl sitting in a school closet with her blue pleated skirt dark with blood? His little girl was growing up; becoming a woman before his eyes, and he stood there before her, dumbfounded, ignorant, and inadequate, with no words of comfort to offer. He wanted to run, to scream, to turn back the hands of time, but it was impossible. Instead he offered her his hand and helped her up and she cried at the sight of him and sobbed his name as if she had lost a pet, "Oh, daddy." He held her elbows and walked behind her to hide the stain, escorting her this way and that to a store and bought her a skirt and guarded the bathroom door while she changed, texting frantic messages to his sister to come immediately. That night neither one spoke of the day's events. They ate in silence and slept early.

"Sorry about that. I thought he was waking." Mae settled back on the corner of her bed in the maid's quarters and pressed a pillow to her free ear to block the sound of their conversation. "What did you want to tell me?"

Rolando sighed. He stood and walked across the floor and looked out a window, tapping the iron bars covering it with his wedding ring. He struggled for the words to describe it, but they wouldn't come. Why didn't she ask about these things? Didn't she know? Didn't she suspect? He suddenly became angry and knit his brow at the darkness and clenched his teeth.

Mae spoke again, interrupting the silence. "Rolando, are you still there? We need to talk as much as possible. This card only has less than thirty minutes left and I won't be able to buy a new one until Sunday. Tell me."

Rolando calmed and gripped the iron bar with his fingers and placed his forehead against the coolness of it. And then he gave up. "Oh, it wasn't that big of a deal. One of her teachers texted some concerns about her feeling sad at school," he lied. "We had a talk about it and she's all right now. It's just that I know talking to you would help out a lot." He knew she would learn of the episode sooner or later and would certainly be upset that he hadn't told her, but for now this would do. And so he sat back down, relieved, and rested his elbows on his knees, leaning into the phone.

"Ok," she replied. "You're right. I do need to talk to her more. I'll buy a card and use all the minutes on her in the next few weeks. We'll talk long and catch up."

"That's good. That will be very good. It will make a difference."

The conversation trailed and stalled again and they both found themselves sitting in silence.

Mae laid back and put the pillow over her face, cocking the cell phone to create a small breathing space. "Did you pay her tuition at St. Mary's?" she asked, knowing that he hadn't. The question was sure to start an argument but she persisted anyway.

"You know I haven't." His voice was already irritated. "We already talked about this. We don't have enough. She'll start at the public school after the semester break in October."

Mae sighed into the phone, a blustery shushing sound amplified by the pillow. "Where does the money go, Rolando?"

He stood and turned away from his daughter, angry now. "You know damn well where it goes. It goes to pay off our debts. It goes for rice. It goes to pay for uniforms and doctors and school projects and cell phone loads and bus fares and everything else it takes just to live. Where do you think it goes?"

Mae was silent. She almost regretted bring it up, but she let the silence linger, a more damning condemnation than anything she could say out loud.

Rolando walked out of the bedroom and across the hall to the kitchen. He lifted a switch and a long florescent bulb buzzed and flickered and popped and eventually came to life in a strobe of flashes. The kitchen was clean. Dishes lay drying on a plastic rack and the smooth counter tiles were scrubbed white. He pinched the phone to his ear with his shoulder and leaned both hands on the counter. "I can't believe you sometimes," he said, his voice rising slightly. "What do you think I do here? Go to movies and gamble on cockfights? Money doesn't go as far as you think. You want receipts? Is that what you want? You want me to mail you a big pile of receipts each month? Would that ease your mind?"

Mae sighed into the phone again. Rolando set his cell phone on the tiled counter and shook his head at it and then picked it up again and put it to his ear. He waited for Mae to say something, but she didn't. "All right," he conceded, flustered and upset at the conversation, "you can expect a big fat envelope of receipts at the end of every month. I hope you look at each one."

"Rolando just stop it."

"Stop what?"

"Stop this. You're blowing things out of proportion. I'm just disappointed that we can't make things work."

"But you think it's because of me. That I'm not doing things right."

"I didn't say that."

"I know you didn't, but it's pretty obvious."

Mae rolled over and lay talking into the pillow, her voice soft and conciliatory. "Rolando I don't think that. I just wonder sometimes if this whole thing wasn't just a big mistake."

Rolando bit his lip and sat in a kitchen chair. Of course it was a mistake, he thought, but he didn't say it. He couldn't. Their sacrifices had to count for something; had to contribute toward something better, something lasting. Otherwise they were just a broken family, limping into the anonymous days ahead of them, the victims of some elaborate scam, mining a field of fool's gold. "We'll be all right," he falsely promised. "We just need to pay off the debts and then we can save." He looked back toward the bedroom and crooked the chairback under his arm. "Besides, college is the most important thing. Our goal should be to save up for her college."

Mae agreed and complimented his thinking. Rolando relaxed. He felt a brief spark in their words, a wisp of things that used to exist between them, like gazing at a photograph of old familiar faces. He basked in the feeling and told her that he missed her, and she said that she loved him, and they smiled together at their phones and let the night fall silent around them.

Rolando stood and flicked the light off and wandered back into his daughter's room. "Her birthday is coming up soon you know. She'll be twelve. She wants a party, but I'm worried about it. I don't know how to make a party for a twelve-year-old girl. She's growing up. Everything I think is nice is for a five-year-old child. She'll be embarrassed."

Mae laughed at the thought of his party planning and tried to console him. "Don't worry, just let her plan it and then invite a lot of people. The party will take shape on its own. It will be fine. Just remember, the more you try to manage it the worse it will get."

Rolando huffed and laughed and finally admitted that was true. "Ah, maybe I'll just get Belen to plan it for me."

Mae sat up abruptly and her face clouded. "What?"

Rolando closed his eyes. He shifted in his seat. He rubbed the phone against his ear to scratch it and then repeated his wife's query for lack of a better response. "What?"

"Belen? Does Belen help you a lot?"

Rolando shook his head at the pale darkness. "No." He opened his eyes and spoke in a measured tone. "I mean, she comes by every once in a while to check on us. Sometimes she brings us food, but that's all. She's been a friend of ours for a long time. She's been good for Christina. You know, a woman. Someone she can talk to." He explained on and his words rambled, but they were unconvincing.

Mae fell silent again, and it lasted for a long time. Rolando didn't break the quiet, but let it sit as Mae did earlier, herding and bullying the conversation onto uncomfortable paths.

Finally she spoke. "Anna says she sees her there a lot."

"Anna's a gossip. She's known for making up rumors and stirring up trouble. You shouldn't listen to anything she says. Why would you waste time even talking to her anyway?"

"Rolando."

"Yes."

Mae breathed into the phone and made a hesitant sound, but it never formed into a word. She sat with her eyes closed and tried to be calm and rational and realistic about their circumstances. "Rolando."

"Yes."

"Rolando, I know that I'm not fulfilling my responsibilities to you as a wife. I know it's hard. I know..."

He stood and turned away from his daughter and exited the room again, unwilling to have such a conversation in her presence. "Mae, look, there's no need to…"

She cut him off. "Listen to me. I know it's hard. I know you're a man. I always knew this kind of thing was a probability with me gone for so long. I just didn't want to think about it."

Rolando grew agitated and marched into the kitchen. He leaned against the counter without turning on the light and held the phone tightly against his ear. "I don't want to have this conversation. You shouldn't listen to other people. They don't know us. They don't know anything. They just like to tell tales. They have no shame."

"Rolando."

"Yes."

"Do you love someone else?"

He considered her words carefully and weighed the significance of each one. "No," he finally declared, and it was true that he didn't. He loved only her.

Mae believed him and lay back again. "Then that's all that matters," she said, a strange sense of resignation sweeping over her.

Rolando felt his eyes well up as the meager lights outside his window blurred and glistened. He wished with all his heart that she was there with him. He desired his wife; both her companionship and her body. He desired her touch and her embrace, the soft caress of her breath on his skin and her frame pressed against him as he slept. But all this was no more than a dream. She was a ghost, an aberration, a whiff and a memory that faded in the daylight and ossified among the static statues of past friends and lovers, only to come to life and then glaciate again, leaving savage pains in her wake.

"Rolando."

"Yes."

"I understand." Her statement was simple. She spoke sympathetically and sincerely, and her words emerged in smooth order. "Just always be sure to put your family first. Don't let our daughter know of these things. I'll be back someday and we'll be a family again. Then none of this will matter. Just remember that and plan on it when you think of the future."

Rolando wiped his eyes with the back of his hand and sniffled away from the phone. "I know. That's all I want too. I want my family together again."

A strange robotic voice interjected over the line. "*You have one minute remaining.*" It was feminine and cold, like a stern nurse announcing the end of visiting hours to distraught family members.

"Rolando."

"Yes."

"Be sure that our daughter sees the good things. Don't let her know the ugly realities of life, not yet. She has a mother who loves her and a father who loves her too. That's what this is about. We have to remember that. It's what makes it all worth it. Do you understand?"

Rolando sniffled and nodded with the phone. "I know." He then turned and went back into the bedroom a final time and sat and stroked his daughter's hair, searching her face carefully for signs of his wife. He studied her lips and the shape of her eyes, her long slender fingers and the perfectly arched hairline, it was a portion of Mae, but not all.

"Mae."

"Yes."

"I love you, Mae."

She let the words settle in and they turned warm in her stomach. It was all she wanted to hear from him, to know that he still loved her, still considered her his wife and partner and the mother of their child; that he had in some measure forgiven her for the pain that tormented him. "Rolando, I ..."

The line cut off and each of them sat in the overwhelming silence, still holding the warm phones to their ears.

⁂

Mae carefully laid the receiver on the telephone and stared at it for a long while. The child in the other room was asleep and didn't need her. She stood and walked through the strange, foreign apartment, looking at the appliances and the pictures and at the furniture. She studied the red, indiscernible Chinese characters and inventoried belongings that were not hers. This wasn't her home. It never would be. She had no home. She went back to her quarters and sat. She cradled a picture of a little girl who existed a long time ago and wept over it like a relic belonging to some deceased relative. Everything was for this little girl, but she couldn't appreciate it. How could she? She didn't exist anymore, and neither did her mother. Someday two strangers would meet at Ninoy Aquino International Airport. They would embrace and smile and struggle through awkward conversations. Perhaps they would become friends, perhaps not. The young woman's life would march forward, taking shape and distinguishing itself in its own way, while the woman's would not. And she cried at the truth of this, silently so as not to wake the child.

⁂

Rolando set the phone down carefully on a wooden table and continued stroking his daughter's hair. He regarded her carefully and she was perfect to him. She was worth all the sacrifice in the world and worth any price they might have to pay. Someday a young woman would exceed the bounds that inhibited her parents and would achieve unthinkable dreams. She would stand tall above her ancestors and make her family proud so that people would remark on her upbringing and her parents and praise them with sincere words. He stared into the darkness and quietly thanked his wife. He thanked God for her and asked for her protection and comfort, and when he was done he crossed himself and kissed his thumb. And time ticked on.

Nora's Better Life

Nora pressed her toes up against the tops of her shoes. She wore new sneakers, silvery gray canvas with blue lines on the side and white shoelaces. Though she adored the sight of them at the store, the new footwear seemed to suffocate her feet and plagued her with intermittent fits of claustrophobia from the ankle down. Nora sat on a narrow bed in the small basement room and suspended her legs out in front of her, trying to spread her toes horizontally this time. Rather an alleviating her discomfort, however, her efforts set off another episode of claustrophobic panic that rippled up her body and caused her to pull at the turtleneck sweater around her neck. She glanced at her *tsinelas*, flip-flops as they were called here, placed neatly inside the closet. She reached down and pulled at one of her laces, undoing the knot. The urge to remove the shoe was overpowering, but she snapped back upright and shook her head. "I have to get used to them sometime," she thought. Though the shoes were uncomfortable and confining, Jim, her fiancé, was adamant that they were necessary. "You're not in the Philippines anymore," he was fond of reminding here.

Nora inhaled deeply as she considered the reality of those words—"not in the Philippines anymore." She looked around the drab makeshift basement bedroom and buried her face in her hands. The irony was that for the past five years she had dreamed of little else than ending up right where she was at—in the United States. She recalled her first night chatting with various foreign men on the internet at an all-night café in Cebu. Though her English was broken and childish and her profile picture blurry, she receive abundant attention. She remembered feeling vulnerable and guilty when many of the men issued vulgar requests or used sexually suggestive word play. Despite her discomfort, however, Nora teased back and never chastised them for their rudeness. After searching multiple sites, Nora was disappointed to discover that very few of her chat partners were ever much younger that forty-five. Most, it seemed, were middle-aged men who had at least one, but often many more, previous marriages, children, and a deep disgust for the materialism and haughty self-centeredness of American women. "Not like you Filipinas," they would often say, "who know how to take care of their men."

It was in one of these chat rooms that Nora first met Jim. She could tell from his profile picture that he was easily twice her tender age of 24, yet, despite the years, there was something that drew Nora to his photo. His eyes seemed soft and inviting somehow. He had a round face, wispy brown thinning hair, and an expression that looked as if he were about to laugh at something. He wore a red sweater over a green button-down shirt. For a long time Nora had assumed his outfit was part of a Christmas ensemble and that the picture must have been snapped at a holiday party. She later learned that it was actually taken in February at Jim's oldest daughter's home in Illinois. Despite this revelation she preferred to continue thinking of it as a jolly Christmas photo. Jim's arms, legs, and the lower two-thirds of his torso were hidden from view in the photo. He did this on purpose to conceal his 48-inch waist. Though Jim excelled at high school athletics in his youth, the years began to catch up with him upon his forty-second birthday, after which he could no longer conceal the signs of his middle age. Jim's profile described him as "single," "traditional," "loving," "fun," and "romantic." These were all qualities that that Nora was looking for, and she assumed that Jim listed them honestly.

Over the next three months their relationship grew via grainy webcam images, crackly voices transmitted thousands of miles, and cartoon-like emoticons, which Nora seemed to use more often than actual words. Her infatuation with Jim was childlike and innocent. She felt like a school girl with a crush on an upper classman. Her girlfriends giggled and teased when she discussed her relationship. "Don't forget us when you're a rich American," they jested, but only partially. The idea appealed to Nora as well, though she would never admit it. "I'm not a gold-digger," she would counter, "besides, Jim is divorced with grown children. He doesn't want another wife. We're just good friends." Nora refused to let herself think of it as anything more. That is, until Jim confessed his love one early morning during a webcam session. He admitted to having fallen madly in love with Nora and asked if it would be all right to visit her and her family in a few months' time. Nora's stomach wrenched at the news with both euphoria and apprehension. What was before only a fairytale, a kind of cyberspace fantasy, had now taken on a firm reality. Nora, of course, agreed, and Jim booked tickets for early June, the beginning of the rainy season.

Jim's arrival in Cebu was much-heralded. Nora brought an entourage of more than twenty people with her to the airport. Cousins, aunts, uncles, and friends from school all milled around the parking lot, sipping Coke from plastic baggies and munching on banana chips. Nora watched the arrival doors carefully. Several middle-aged foreigners emerged, but none looked like the man from the chat rooms. Suddenly a heavy-set man in beige shorts and a white polo shirt waved enthusiastically in her direction. Nora hesitated, squinting her eyes against the sun to scrutinize the apparent acquaintance. Having caught her eye, Jim waved more vigorously. Nora sucked in a deep breath. He didn't look at all like the man from the internet. He was so old, so stout, so out of place with his stark white calves and reddish face. Nora tried to picture herself next to him, but no images came. She suddenly felt terribly embarrassed in front of her family and friends. Why hadn't she come in private? Why did she tell everyone about his impending arrival? Nora closed her eyes and when she opened them again she forced her face into a big smile. "Hello Jim," she called, waving back at the stranger. Jim picked up black suitcase and rushed over while Nora remained still.

"I can't believe I'm finally here," he exclaimed, wrapping Nora in a smothering embrace. Nora turned her head, placing her ear against Jim's chest. He smelled of a type of spiced soap she didn't recognize. She felt a slight dampness to his shirt. His face was already beaded with perspiration and his thinning hair matted to his head.

Nora pulled away and felt his curly arm hair tickle the back of her hand. "I can't believe it either. How was your trip?"

"Long," he responded, admiring Nora's face, a broad smile shaping his lips. "You are so beautiful in person." Nora nodded curtly and turned, scanning a long line of multicolored cabs parked along a nearby curb. Jim attempted another embrace but Nora quickly stepped back and waved at one of the taxis. These fleeting seconds were all that she needed to allow her entourage to converge, saving her from another episode of awkward public intimacy with this stranger. Jim politely greeted each person and joked about the heat and wiped his face with his sleeve. The group smiled and laughed in unison at the novel foreigner and offered whatever English phrases they had been practicing until an airport security guard herded them toward the waiting taxies. Nora stood patiently on the curb and watched until Jim climbed into the back seat with his black Samsonite suitcase. She then swooped deftly into the front seat. "I have to watch the meter," she explained, smiling politely and glancing at the driver.

Nora's family lived in a gray hollow-block house with corrugated tin roofing and a cement floor some twenty-five kilometers outside the city. It sat anonymously among other similar dwellings clustered between rice fields in various stages of planting. It was simple and unimpressive, but quaint and welcoming just the same. Jim chatted constantly as the vehicle chugged and stopped and lurched forward through the city traffic. Nora kept silence except to acknowledge his words when absolutely necessary. Her reticence unnerved Jim, but his smile remained.

There were at least as many people waiting in and around the house to greet Jim as there were at the airport. Nora's mother, Isabel, stood just outside the front door, surrounded by an assortment of relatives and curious neighbors who gawked and laughed and craned their necks at the approaching car. She had been waiting for this day as well. Isabel not only approved, but actively encouraged Nora's online relationship with Jim. Each morning when Nora returned from her internet café conversations, Isabel would flood her with questions and encouragements about her internet love affair. It was a vicarious endeavor. Nora's mother had also engaged in a relationship with an American as a young woman in the late seventies. The two met in a disco in Cebu City in 1977. Isabel had given herself to him freely, spending every night of his two-week stay at his hotel downtown. After the man returned to the States the pair exchanged dozens of letters for nearly two months. After that, however, the correspondence became more and more infrequent and eventually stopped altogether. Isabel loved Nora's father, but always considered her failed long-distance relationship a missed opportunity.

The taxi rolled to a stop in front of the crowded house and sat idling in the afternoon heat. The meter read just under 300 pesos. Jim handed the driver a thousand peso bill and told him to keep the change—something he would do repeatedly during his visit whenever paying for anything and everything. He seemed to have no other denominations in his wallet except for the obnoxious blue and white bills, still crisp from their limited circulation. Whether paying for a week's supply of rice for Nora's family or buying a coke at the local *sari-sari* store, Jim always placed a thousand peso bill on the counter and told the proprietors to "keep the change" in an indifferent tone. This fact alone seemed to immediately endear him to most of the curious neighbors and extended family. His generosity and wealth seemed boundless. The monetary notes appeared to be nothing more than mere paper to him, and he disseminated them freely, never speaking of their worth. Nora was not impressed. Jim's apparent disregard for value made her feel cheap and commodified, as if she were being bought as well.

Jim's first week was a blur of excursions to Cebu's famous attractions—the Basilica Minore Del Santo Nino, beach outings at Mactan and Tambuli resorts, dinner at Alejandro's Filipino Resto on Don Jose Avila Street, and nightly outings to videoke clubs and dancing halls—all paid for by Jim without thought. Sometimes there were as many as twenty-five people tagging along with the couple. Jim rented Jeepneys and taxis to transport the assemblage from place to place and always made sure that there were enough meals, drinks, and snacks to go around. Despite her reservations, Nora found the outings pleasant enough. As long as she and Jim were not alone and nothing too intimate transpired between them, Nora felt comfortable. Each night after the day's activities, Nora gave Jim a friendly hug and then walked into the house with her relatives without looking back, leaving her suitor in a taxi bound for his hotel.

Jim's second week in Cebu was much different than his first, however. One Tuesday evening after returning from a karaoke club, Jim explained to Nora that he didn't want to go out anymore; that he only wanted to spend time with her and her family. Nora felt an uneasiness rise in her stomach. She strained to think of other interesting places they could go, enthusiastically pitching each idea. But he would have none of it. The following days were long and awkward. Jim sat around the house sweating and drinking coke and talking with Nora's mother mostly. The two seemed to hit is off quite well. There were, after all, only four years separating their respective ages. In a moment of idle reflection, Nora even thought that they made a handsome couple sitting there on the rattan couch under a wooden carving of the Last Supper. She immediately felt guilty, though, and chastised herself for ever entertaining such a notion, but there it was before her just the same.

Nora spent most her time thinking up chores and errands to minimize her awkward moments with Jim. He offered to hire someone to wash the clothes, which was always done by hand, but Nora refused, claiming that she didn't trust anyone to get her garments as clean as she could. He even retreated on his initial declaration and suggested that they eat out at night, so Nora wouldn't have to spend time at the market and cooking. She again refused, claiming that restaurant food upset her stomach. And Jim's consternation grew.

After tolerating three days of her daughter's artful avoidance, Isabel pulled Nora into a bedroom at the back of the house and demanded a change. "He has come all this way to see you, and this is how you treat him?" Her Visayan was quick and angry, unintelligible to Jim sitting in the front room. "If you didn't like him then you shouldn't have led him on!" Nora looked away and shook her head. Isabel grabbed her daughter's chin with her thumb and forefinger and jerked her face back into position. "He thinks that you want to marry him. He has come all this way and spent all this money because he assumed you were committed to being with him. He is nice and will take care of you. It's time for you to grow up!" Nora fought back tears and bit her lip and glared at her mother, but in the end, she simply nodded in agreement. Isabel softened her expression and brushed Nora's hair back from her eyes. "I'm telling you this because I love you,

Nora," she explained. "I want what's best for you. You are so young and have no idea how difficult life can be. Jim is a good man. Give him a chance." Nora remained silent as hot tears streamed down her cheeks. "Trust me," Isabel urged, kissing her daughter on the forehead, "I'll always do what's best for you."

Jim's remaining days were much different. Nora wiled away the hours sitting next to her visitor on the rattan couch, talking about inconsequential things, posing banal questions about his upbringing and his likes and dislikes and his plans for the future. Jim noticed her changed attitude and interpreted it as an invitation to become more affectionate. He began taking Nora's hand when they walked or placing his arm around her while sitting down. Isabel noticed as well and made sure the couple had all the privacy they might need to explore their physical intimacy. Soon Jim was stealing kisses and stroking her thighs, tracing the contours of her midsection and nuzzling her neck. One night, Jim asked Nora to come back to his hotel. He whispered seductively and pulled her body close to his. Nora blew air roughly through her nostrils and pinched her eyes shut at the proposition. The thought of surrendering her virginity in a hotel room to this man repulsed her. She knew that everyone already assumed the deed was done, and this repulsed her even more. She stared defiantly and raged at him in her mind, but outwardly she only politely refused. Jim moped and huffed and shook his head, but in the end it was hopeless and he consoled himself with the thought that she couldn't refuse him forever.

Everyone seemed to heartily endorse the union, and expressed nothing but congratulations and praise. The only one apparently not on the bandwagon was Nora's father, Danilo. He avoided Jim whenever possible, spending countless hours behind the house tending to a collection of young mango trees or fussing over his brightly-colored fighting cocks tallied to short V-shaped shelters. In the evenings he gathered with his friends in front of a little sari-sari store down the street and drank Ginebra gin with San Miguel beer to dull the day's events. He never spoke of the large Caucasian frequenting his house or of his daughter's relationship with him. During the first couple days of his visit, Jim often ventured out back to make inquiries about the majestic-looking cocks or the advantages of fumigating the mango trees with smoke, but Danilo only nodded curtly when absolutely necessary and never said more than a dozen words. Eventually Jim quit trying, and instead concentrated on endearing himself to the rest of the family. At night, Nora could hear her parents arguing quietly in the darkness. Her mother's whispers were angry and punctuated. Her father's replies were short and melancholy. Often his only response to Isabel's ranting was a quiet plea: "This is not right for our girl. She doesn't want this, can't you see?" Isabel would huff and cut him with insults, and then there was silence. Nora cried at each instance, her quite sobs filling up the darkness until sleep overtook her.

On his last night, Jim insisted on taking everyone out to dinner at Anzani, one of Cebu's most exclusive restaurants in the Lahung Nivel Hills area. Nora and Isabel wore gaudy spaghetti strap gowns with black sequins and white silk ribbons. Though they sauntered somewhat clumsily in their high-heeled shoes, both women looked stunning. Nora felt conspicuous by it all. Isabel carried herself proudly, constantly dabbing the sweat beading on her face and wiping her neck and chest in delicate motions. Even Danilo wore a new pineapple fiber *barong* with intricately embroidered coconut trees and native designs down the front, and black slacks tailored just for the occasion. Initially, he objected to the ostentatious garments, but was quickly reprimanded by Isabel, who cruelly reminded him that he had never provided her with such an extravagant outing, and that he should not deny his daughter this experience.

The restaurant was formal and dimly-lit. Businessmen chatted and lovers whispered in the soft candlelight. They were met at the door by an impeccable waiter in white shirt, black bowtie, and slacks. He was a handsome young Filipino with thick black hair and prominent cheekbones. He smiled at

Nora as the throng filed past him and he watched her among the group. The young man took great care to seat each of the ladies present, making the process as formal and special as possible. He stood behind Nora and gently pushed her chair in as she leaned back and felt the top of his smooth hand against her bare back for the briefest moment. The touch sent a thrill through her body and she immediately ached for it again. She imagined the soft feel of his kiss; she yearned to take his hand and run out of the restaurant in a fit of reckless passion. She closed her eyes and imagined the scene, letting it play out slowly in small details. Sensing her emotions, the boy lingered at her chair and their flesh touched again. Jim glanced sideways at the couple. Unsettled by their proximity, he cleared his throat and placed a thick reddish hand on Nora's thigh. The waiter snapped his gaze upward immediately and continued his circle around the table. The thrill in Nora's stomach turned to nausea as she glared at Jim's hand. Thick and heavy, it weighed on her like an anvil; a symbol of her bondage.

Dinner was a boisterous affair with relentless chatter, loud laughter, and multiple toasts to the couple's future. Nora forced a smile but said very little. She stole occasional glances at the waiter, but the young man was determined to avoid her now. How could he compete with a rich American? As the night drew to a close, Jim became increasingly withdrawn, as if contemplating some deep philosophical question. Finally, at a little past nine-thirty, he stood and asked for quiet. Speaking more to the gathering than to Nora, he confessed that he had fallen deeply in love with the woman seated at his side. He recounted the details of their long distance courtship and gushed about his romantic feelings. His words were sincere, but soon they dragged on and became repetitive. After what seemed to Nora like hours of inchoate ramblings, Jim reached into his pocket and retrieved a small black box. He opened it and presented its contents. The crowd gasped and then oohed in unison at the golden engagement ring studded with a glittering half-carat diamond.

The only one still silent was Nora. Her chest constricted as she choked back sobs. The manifest emotions provoked another flurry of ooohs and awhs, but her face contorted in agonizing ways and the dinner guests looked away.

Jim sat back in his chair and pushed the black box in Nora's direction. "I love you, Nora. Will you be my wife?" The table grew silent except for the whispered gulps of Nora's suppressed sobs. She glanced at her parents. The contrast between them was devastating. Her father sat slumped down in his chair, his expression defeated and his eyes glassy. Isabel quivered with joy and nodded sharply at her daughter, a silent command to accept the ring, and then smiled dramatically at Jim.

The trembling young woman reached out and took the box as the table erupted into applause. Nora stared at the ring, its sparkling jewel distorted by the light refracting through her tears. "You've made me so happy!" Jim exclaimed, placing his hands on Nora's shoulders. He pulled her close and pressed his mouth against her lifeless lips. More hoots and applause echoed from around the table. Nora blushed with humiliation. Her stomach wretched and her throat constricted. She rushed awkwardly to the bathroom where she vomited her 1200 peso dinner into the toilet. And the party carried on.

The next seven months were a blur of complicated preparations. Passport applications and government clearances, interviews at the embassy and wedding arrangements kept Nora's days full and fleeting. At the beginning of each month, she would climb aboard one of the creaking, multi-colored, non-air conditioned buses that looped down near the Western Union on General Maxilom Avenue. She would fill out yellow and white forms and accepted Jim's remittances without expression while the teller chirped prying questions. Nora usually offered no reply to the nosy cashier other than to request that her payment be made in pesos rather than dollars. She would grab the obscene pile of light blue and orange bills and stuff it haphazardly into her handbag, never counting it. She came to detest the wad of paper in her purse and despised the surge of popularity and admiration it solicited from her friends and family. Her disdain for the bills was just as well, however, since Isabel immediately took possession of cash when Nora brought it home. She didn't know where her mother put it or what she spent it on; she didn't care.

One by one the pieces fell into place until the day of Nora's departure arrived. Once again, a cumbersome congregation of family and friends filled the airport parking lot. Their mood was festive despite the impending separation. Nora nodded politely as friends and kin wished her good luck and asked her not to forget them. Her heart ached, but it was a familiar ache, something she had grown accustomed to over the past several months. No tears filled her eyes and no sobs bubbled to the top of her throat. She was resigned, numb to the anxieties needling her brain. Little by the little the crowds backed away, allowing Nora some final moments with her parents. Isabel's face was streaked with tears, but she wore a smile and her motions were animated and giddy. Nora stood motionless as her mother embraced her tightly. "I'm so happy for you," she whispered, pressing her glistening cheek against Nora's neck. "I know, Mama," she stated flatly and pulled away, feigning a slight smile. In some ways, escaping Isabel's critical eye was the only bright spot in Nora's otherwise gray-toned world.

After several more hugs and well wishes, Nora turned toward Danilo. His position was guarded with his arms folded tightly over his chest. He craned his head sharply to the side as if straining to see beyond some distant obstruction. His breathing was short and staccatoed, but measured as if he were concentrating on it. Nora took as step closer, bridging the short distance between them. Danilo let his arms fall to his sides and shifting his gaze to the ground. Though he tried to hide it from her, Nora could clearly see his glistening eyes and discerned the hot tears streaming down his russet cheeks. She looked longingly at her pitiful father. His hands shook and his lips contorted as he struggled violently to suppress his emotions. Nora inhaled deeply, and then, without warning, her emotions broke loose as well. The fear and pain raging inside of her gushed out as she threw her arms around her father's neck and clung to him like a frightened child. She sobbed uncontrollably into his chest and whispered nonsense into his shirt and spoke his name again and again. She felt the lean sinew of his muscles and took in the smell of his clothes. This was her father, the only man she truly loved and trusted; the only one who had appeared the least bit concerned about her fears; the only reasonable voice among a cacophony of others calling for her to prostitute herself out for a "better life." She squeezed him tighter and imagined she was his little girl again—a little girl Danilo had the power to save, to comfort, to tell stories to, to love unconditionally. Danilo returned his daughter's embrace with equal desperation. He let his tears flow freely and without shame as he held her. Memories of Nora's childhood flooded his mind as well. He recalled a small girl in a broad blue pleated skirt and white blouse meandering around the rice fields on her way home from the second grade. He watched as she ventured out into the slippery mud and itchy rice stalks to be with her father despite his warnings and certain chastisements from Isabel. He held her hand and swung her over small ditches, striving to keep her school uniform clean, while she grasped at insects and shouted greetings to an old water buffalo grazing nearby. Danilo remembered the same little girl nestled silently on a small bamboo bed, her arms wrapped around pillow as she slept in the early morning light. She was the picture of sweet innocence, the embodiment of everything that was pure and precious about the world. His stomach suddenly wretched in between sobs as he considered her impending defilement at the hands of the foreigner, her innocence destroyed. His mind burned with rage that escaped in the form of tears. He wished death upon Jim and cursed his wife for their evil schemes and heartless betrayals. He suddenly hated everyone alive except Nora. His soul drowned in the boiling emotions and then his mind fell silent. He gently released his daughter, whispered "I love you" one final time, and then turned and walked away without looking back.

&

Nora swung her head from side to side, shaking out the unpleasant memories, but they were too vivid to dispel completely. She reached down and pulled off her new shoes. They sat heavy and awkward in her hands. She tossed them haphazardly in the corner and then stretched out her toes horizontally. The socks still felt constraining, but at least she could move. It took less than a minute, however, and Nora peeled the socks off as well. She stood and gripped the carpet with her toes and felt the cool air caress her feet. She closed her eyes and breathed in. The basement was musty and stale. She imagined the smell of the rice fields after the rain and the cool monsoon breezes once the winds had shifted southward. She imagined her father strolling along the narrow mounts of dirt separating the saturated patties. Her throat suddenly jerked and she opened her eyes to dispel the emotion. She had convinced herself she was past this now. No more crying.

"Nora," a deep feminine voice shot down the stairs like a bolt of electricity. Nora jolted. "Lunch is ready, Nora. We're all waiting for you." The voice belonged to Jim's younger sister Janis, a heavy-set woman in her mid-forties with chemically induced red hair and large round eyes. Though she was relatively advanced in age for bearing children, Janis had given birth to twin boys only two years earlier. The children were rambunctious and rough, uncouth boys that demonstrated little regard for others or their possessions. Jim had originally hoped that Janis and Nora would become close friends, but it hadn't worked out that way. Though there was no outward animosity between them, Nora sensed that Janis somehow resented her relationship with Jim. She had once hinted to some friends that Nora was probably a gold-digger. Though Nora pretended not to understand her sister-in-law's hushed English, she knew well what the term meant and the accusation hurt. "Nora," the voice bellowed again, exuding a familiar aggravated tone, "We're all waiting for you." Panic flooded her mind. Without thought, she scrambled to the closet, slipped her feet into the *tsinelas* and hurried up the stairs.

"Here she is," Janis announced in dramatic fashion. "Let the party begin." The twins were seated in identical highchairs at the far end of an oblong oak table. The rowdy pair munched on cheese sandwiches and Cheetoes. Somehow mayonnaise and cheese dust had already spread across their faces and into their light blond hair. Nora chose a seat at the opposite end of the table near Jim's mother. Though she was formally announced, those seated at the table hardly took notice of her. Compared to the massive European-Americans seated around her, Nora took up very little space. Even Jim's mother, at a smallish 5'2 and 135 pounds, seemed to tower over Nora's slight build. Nora's posture made her look even smaller. She sat with her shoulders hunched and knees together, with her hands folded in her lap. She liked it this way. Like an unnoticed observer watching her new life from the outside, Nora sat silently; afraid the objects of her scrutiny would become suddenly aware of her gaze.

Janis stood behind the kitchen counter inventorying a row of sandwiches, ensuring that each was properly assembled and accompanied by the right brand of chips. Jim and his white-haired father, Gary, were engrossed in a discussion of sports teams while Margaret, Jim's mother, a heavily-wrinkled woman with a yellowish tan and bleached hair, sat scanning the pages of a "Parade Magazine" inserted into that day's newspaper. Nora watched them all carefully, as a psychiatrist might observe patients from behind a two-way mirror. Their routines and interests, conversations and habits all seemed so oddly foreign to her. This was family time, and yet, the social atmosphere felt arid and hollow to her. They all looked like important people living important lives, but to Nora there was something curiously unreal and trivial about it all. She turned her gaze out a broad window beyond the table. Yellow and orange leaves quaked in the autumn breeze. The decaying foliage struck her as both beautiful and foreboding. She watched a large leaf detach and then spin and pitch as it descended to the grass below.

"My goodness child!" The voice pierced the silence like a hot knife. Nora turned to her mother-in-law wide-eyed. "Where in the world are your socks and shoes?" she asked in the same shrill tone. Nora felt a ripple of fear run through her torso. She shook her head slowly, unable to think of any words in response. Margaret gave a disapproving look. "Don't you know it's only going to be in the 40s today? Bare feet on this tile floor will surely make you sick. What are you thinking?" Nora felt her face burn with embarrassment. She wanted to cover it with her hands, to hide from the unbearable shame, but she knew that would only make things worse. These people demanded to be acknowledged when they spoke. Nora looked to Jim for support, but Margaret beat her there. "I thought you were going to buy this girl some real shoes." She sounded exasperated, exhausted by the absurdity of it all. "You can't have her running around like she still lives in the tropics."

Jim chuckled at his mother's remark. He looked at Nora with a confused expression. "Where are your shoes, dear? I thought you had them on earlier." Nora forced a smile and shook her head. She still couldn't get the words to come. How could she explain her claustrophobia? Her need for liberation? Her anxiety at being held so tightly by the suffocating footwear? She didn't know how to fully express her feelings in Visayan, much less English. She felt tears begin to well up in her eyes as anger swept over her. She shook her head again and tried to maintain the smile, but tears were already streaming out of the corners of her eyes. Everyone in the room, including the twins, sat quietly, watching her devastation unfold. After a seeming eternity, Nora let out a muffled, anguished high-pitched groan. Mortified, she finally covered her face with both hands and rushed from the room.

Margaret gave Jim an innocent shrug. "Did I say something?" Jim made a face. "I'm just concerned about her health," Margaret defended. "Jeez, it certainly wasn't anything to cry about."

Janis sighed from behind the kitchen counter. "That's what happens when you marry a child."

"That's enough, Janis." Jim's tone became angry. "You are way out of line. I know how you feel about this whole situation. You don't need to be snide about it."

Gary put his arm around his son. "Now Jim," he began in a fatherly voice that had mediated a thousand disputes between his children, "don't be angry with Janis. It was a rude remark" —he shot a disapproving look in her direction, "but Nora had no reason to cry about such an insignificant comment." He squeezed his son's shoulder and offered a brief closed-mouth smile. "Now, go in there and make your wife feel better. Your mom didn't mean anything by her observation. We sometimes forget how hard this must be for Nora. Life is different in advanced countries like ours. She probably doesn't know how to act with such nice new things suddenly piled on her. Give her some time."

Jim rose and left the table. "There," Gary declared triumphantly. "Now let's get back to enjoying lunch." Margaret was already reabsorbed in her "Parade Magazine" and Janis struggled with the twins. Life continued as usual despite the awkward moment.

Jim found her in the living room. She stood slouched over staring out a large bay window into the Michigan woods beyond the driveway. He could tell by her stillness that she had finished crying. He approached slowly and placed his heavy hand on her shoulder. "Do you feel better?" Nora didn't respond. "You know my mother didn't mean to embarrass you or hurt your feelings earlier. She's just concerned about you." Nora didn't move. "Please look at me, Nora." Jim became impatient. "This is such a silly thing. Let's not make a big deal of it." Nora took in a studdered breath but did not turn around. Jim tightened his grip on her shoulder and turned her body firmly. Her eyes widened in alarm at the strength of his touch. She resisted only briefly, but then turned submissive in his grip. "That's better," Jim said, softening his expression. "Now, I want you to listen to me. I know this is hard for you. I know you are far from home. This is your first time to a new country. You are surrounded by new things and new people. I'm sure you miss your family and friends, but you have a new family now." Jim stroked her face softly. "Those people in there love you and want you to be a part of their lives. You just have to give it some effort and courage. You can't come to pieces over every little thing." Nora sniffled and dabbed her eyes with her sleeve. She wanted to turn away, but feared his grip. Jim searched her face carefully and forced her into an embrace holding her rigid body for several seconds until she softened. He then gently kissed her forehead. "Now, go on downstairs and put on your shoes and hurry back up for lunch. Janis made you a turkey sandwich. I think you'll love it. I promise we'll make some rice for dinner." Jim bent down, making his face equal with hers. "Ok?" Nora forced a smile and nodded. "Ok," Jim answered for her and patted her back like a child.

Nora walked back through the kitchen on her way to the basement. Margaret, Gary, and Janis all wore large dramatic smiles. Gary nodded for no apparent reason as she passed, but no one spoke. Nora smiled back and quickly descended the stairs to the basement. She could hear their muffled voices following after her, but she couldn't make out their comments and speculations. Nora gathered up her socks and shoes and slipped the appropriate foot into each item. The claustrophobia immediately returned; more suffocating and overpowering than ever. But Nora did not resist it now. She embraced it; she let it flood over her body and overwhelm her mind. She hoped it would suffocate the screams of agony and rage in her brain. She pulled the shoelaces tight until she could feel them cutting into her foot through the canvas. She then secured the bows with a double knot, just like Jim had taught her, and jerked the laces taunt. She dreaded going back upstairs, having to face them again, those people who judged her to be so inadequate to her new surroundings, an opportunist, a child, a tropical native. But there was nothing left to be done. It couldn't be avoided. There was no alternative, no way out. And so Nora turned and dutifully ascended the stairs to her new "better life," the shoes pinching painfully against her feet with each step.

The Hard Decisions

He came again last night, but I don't know why. Some say the dead visit us in our dreams to impart messages or warnings or words of comfort. My Grandmother used to say that the spirits swirl about us in constant concern, watching this or that and attempting to influence the course of our lives. They can be kind or terrifying; angels of light or horrifying nightmares in the darkness. They take whatever form they must to bestow their otherworldly wisdom on us mortals. I don't know if this is the case, but I do know the dreams are growing more profound, more urgent. He has come three nights in a row now. I am left disturbed, unsettled in the morning, unable to shake the feelings that typically evaporate only seconds after waking. I carry them with me throughout the day and they weigh heavily on my mind before sleeping again at night. And yet, somehow I don't want them to stop. There is substance in them. Something meant for me that I cannot discern.

Last night my Lolo stood on the banks of a rice patty. It was my father's father, as always. He was dressed like a peasant in the old way. He wore a coarse off-white shirt with three buttons left open and khaki canvas pants cut off at the middle of his shins. A broad hat woven from palm fibers sat crooked on his head and his feet were bare. He was old and tired looking. His brown leathery skin creased and sagged, and the bones in his cheeks, arms and hands protruded conspicuously. He looked at me for a long time with a kind of critical expression, but never spoke a word.

It occurred to me shortly how strange the entire scenario was. The rice field was an old family plot that I recognized well, but that hadn't been farmed in over ten years. It didn't even belong to the family anymore, sold off some years ago after my Lolo's death. Last time I saw it, it was covered in tangled weeds and cogon grass except for circular patches where bony cattle and stout water buffaloes grazed around the poles to which they were tethered. The plot seemed out of context as well. There were stilted houses set about it and clusters of coconut trees that didn't exist in actuality, and the colors were off somehow. It seemed as if I was looking at an earlier time, but one that I wouldn't recognize from memory. The strangest part, however, was my Lolo. He'd been dead now for nearly thirteen years, and I told him as much standing there before me. This revelation didn't seem to faze him in the slightest. He still wore the same critical expression. We continued to stare at each other and then suddenly he waded down into the muddy patty and dug into the silt and hoisted great lumps of it up to fortify the bank. His white sleeves hung heavy with the brownish water and splashed when he put his arms in. I watched him for a while and then my heart began to ache. I walked up the narrow bank and squatted down in front of him.

"You don't have to do this anymore, Lolo," I told him. "We don't farm this land anymore. There's no money in it. We don't even own it anymore."

The old man paused for only a second without looking up and then reached back down into the primordial soup and scooped out some more sediment and patted it into place against the dyke.

The sorrow in me grew. I began to become desperate for him to understand. I reached out and put my hand on his shoulder and he halted. "You don't have to do this anymore," I repeated. "There's no need." I reached down and tugged at my button-down shirt. "I live in America now. In Los Angeles. I send money every month. Do you understand?"

The old man remained quiet for several seconds and then looked up. His arms were dripping and the mud on his sleeves had begun to crust. He nodded slowly, as tears sprung to his eyes. The boundless melancholy swirling in those black glistening eyes overwhelmed me with a sense of sadness that I cannot begin to express. I tried to say something comforting, but there was nothing to say. And then I woke up.

❧

Carlos stepped out of Ninoy Aquino International Airport and into a light drizzle that wet his blue striped Van Heusen shirt and beaded on his black suitcase. He breathed in the sour, musty smell of the city and coughed into his fist. It had been almost three years since he'd been back. He didn't take time to look around, but walked instantly to the front of a line of battered cabs and crawled into the back seat with his suitcase sitting beside him. "Take me to the bus terminal in Cubao," he said in English and rode the rest of the way in silence.

The bus teetered and swayed and creaked as it drove through the late night Manila traffic. It stopped twice on its way to La Union, once in Tarlac and once more in Carmen, Pangasinan. Each time he pretended to sleep with his head lying against the window while pushy young men in cut-off Levis and bony, hunch-backed women strolled up and down the aisles selling pork rinds, peanuts, and quail eggs. When the bus continued on, he simply stared out the window past his reflection into the blackness until his eyes grew heavy and he finally nodded off.

It was sometime in the early morning when they pulled to a stop in a dusty gravel lot twelve kilometers north of San Fernando City. The driver killed the engine and the bus rattled and jerked and eventually fell silent. Carlos woke suddenly, unsettled by the quiet. He looked out the window and scanned the landscape for familiar sights. He found many. There had been very little change in the small provincial town since his last visit. The same rows of wooden shacks composing the market stood where they had years before without signs of repair or improvement. The old church tower rose prominently in the distance. Its once sharp corners had crumpled and it was still without a bell. The elementary school, the canteens, the seed stores and the tire repair shops; they all still looked the same.

The morning air was cool and smelled of wet concrete and wood smoke. He pulled and twisted his roller suitcase over the gravel and hoisted it up onto a crude metal rack made from rebar and welded to a tricycle sidecar. "Barangay Legaspi," he directed. "Just behind the vista chapel, past the barangay hall." The driver kick-started his bike and sputtered off into the morning mist.

There was no one there to greet him when Carlos arrived. He didn't tell anyone he was coming. "There are too many expectations if I do," he explained to an American colleague a few nights before. "If I tell them I'm coming, they'll start asking me to bring Ivory soap and Dove lotion and Pringles and Levis and heaven knows what else. If I just show up it won't be an issue."

He stood for a long while surveying a cement house with corrugated tin roofing and iron grates over the windows. It has been painted a dull yellow since his last visit and someone had added a small concrete patio out front and embedded a dozen or more one peso coins into the shape of a cross into it. It was bordered with an impressive array of potted orchids in various stages of bloom. The bare patch of dirt surrounding the structure was swept clean except for a few dozen golden leaves that had fallen during the night. He studied the wispy crosshatch of brush marks in the dirt and looked at the pattern of the leaves on the ground as if they contained some concealed message. It was quaint and cozy and, for Carlos, uninspiring.

He walked in without knocking and set his suitcase just inside the door and stepped into the kitchen and leaned against the doorframe without speaking. It was several seconds before his mother looked up and screamed in surprise and joy. She hugged him and kissed his face and wiped tears with the back of her hand until he told her to stop.

"Why didn't you call us?" she asked, holding his hand like a child and forcing him to sit in a white plastic chair.

He smiled and then shook his head and lied. "I didn't know until the last moment I'd be able to come. I found a last-minute deal on the internet." It felt strange speaking Ilokano, though it still flowed easily.

His mother nodded in complete understanding and stroked his hand. "It doesn't matter. I'm just glad you're here." She looked out a small window over the sink. "Your father and brother left early. They are preparing the fields. Planting will come any day now." She brightened. "Why don't you go out there and surprise them? They'd be so happy to see you. It will bring back memories."

Carlos's face clouded. "I don't think so, Ma. I'm tired from the trip." He stood and arched his back. "I think I just want to take a shower and sleep for a little while."

She stood as well. "Of course, son. You get settled in." She took his hand again, hoping he would sit for a while, but he didn't, and so she let him go.

He stripped and pumped water into a bucket from an old cast iron spigot protruding out of a cement slab. The cold liquid streamed over his body and splashed on the coarse concrete in waves. He shivered and blew a misty spray out of his mouth and nose and stood naked for a long while in the corrugated tin closet. When he finished he dressed in shorts and a plain white t-shirt, and then crawled into his brother's bed, since he no longer had one of his own. He lay on his side staring at the pinkish walls as the electric fan swept back and forth, drying his hair and clearing the remaining beads of water on his exposed flesh. A little more than an hour later he heard his father and brother return. He listened to his mother tell them the news and then he closed his eyes and pretended to sleep.

Carlos spent much of his first week visiting with extended family, old friends and former classmates. He explained the nature of his work time and time again, and artfully dodged questions about his love life. When he grew tired of the conversations or someone began to hint at favors, he would simply excuse himself and walk away. His father and brother spent their days in the fields, and Carlos spent his evenings at an internet café pretending to answer emails for work. They never pressed him or questioned his priorities. They just let him go and spoke with him when they could. His brother teased and laughed whether Carlos liked it or not, but no meaningful conversations took place. His father asked him about his work and his apartment and about the flight and his used Honda Civic and things he heard about America in the news. Carlos divulged pertinent details but never asked questions about his father's life in return. What was there to ask? There wasn't much to it that he could see. The old man grew rice and vegetables and slept and ate and listened to Bombo Radio on the weekends. He occasionally attended mass or festivals on special holidays, but that was the extent of his adventures. He existed. There was nothing significant in it that Carlos could determine; nothing bright or hopeful or mysterious. It was virtually the same life lived by billions of others who whiled away their years and then died. At times Carlos despised it, and in deep places he hated himself for that, which made him despise it all the more. And so he avoided his father altogether, preferring transparent excuses to uncomfortable conversation.

Eventually, however, he ran out of reasons to stay away. He found himself sitting on the family's rattan couch whiling away the slow hot afternoons watching variety shows and commercials for cell phones on an old color TV. He felt like a foreign guest who had run out of sites to see and now sat in a dank hotel watching mindless television programs and cursing himself for wasting his money.

"Why don't you go down and visit your father and brother in the fields?" his mother urged. He couldn't think of a reason not to and so he rose and made his way around the house toward the vast expanse of patchwork patties that lay over the countryside like some massive quilt spread over the tropical earth.

He trod the narrow embankments and zigged and zagged left and right at ninety-degree angles trying to avoid the wet earth. He could see the pair off in the distance. They toiled in the mud and the heat alongside a massive water buffalo. He stopped and studied them from a distance; their broad hats and thin bodies hidden under long-sleeved tees and cuffed canvas pants. He thought that this is how it must have looked a thousand years ago—peasants laboring away for their subsistence; never knowing of the world outside, ignorant of the luxuries and technologies that blessed the rest of the world's inhabitants. He shook his head and spit in the mud, and then walked on toward the thin figures in the distance.

He found a soft grassy knoll a ways off and sat with his knees bent at sharp angles. His brother saw him immediately. He waved and stepped out of the mud, stomping mightily to shake off the black paste and then walked over and sat beside his brother. Their father continued trudging through the mud behind a water buffalo harnessed to an iron harrow that raked and cut the wet soil into a fine silt.

"Glad you made it out finally. I don't suppose you'd like to help."

Carlos grunted out a chuckle and shook his head.

His brother straightened out one leg and then bent it back. The mud had begun to dry and crust around his knee and it crumbled off in tiny clods as he moved. "I think we'll have a good harvest this year. Prices are up."

Carlos turned and stared at his brother grimly with one eye squinted. "What do you all do with the money I send? Something's wrong if you have to keep working this hard."

His brother shifted and brushed some mud off his sleeve and stared out over the fields. "Well, it takes money for seed and fertilizer. And we always have to hire someone at harvest time. And then there's milling and…" His voice trailed off.

"In other words you waste it." Carlos's voice was unexpectedly hard and accusatory.

His brother offered no reply.

Carlos continued, seizing on the opportunity to vent as his words devolving into a rant. "I don't understand it. You and Papa pour the money into this sinkhole, and for what? I work hard and drive an old car and scrimp and save like a miser abroad so you can have better lives. And do you? No! You're no better off than you've ever been. Nothing's improved. Nothing's changed. You continue to struggle and live like ignorant peasants. Damn it!"

His brother wrapped both arms around a bent leg and watched the countryside quietly. The words stung, but he didn't respond to them. It would only make matters worse. Besides, what was there to say? They did pour the money into the earth. They did live like peasants. He didn't seem to see the problem with this, but then again he was "ignorant," and so he remained silent.

Carlos watched him and then let out a disgusted sigh. "Do you understand what I am saying?"

His brother nodded and lied for the sake of peace. "Yes, I understand."

But peace didn't come. "Then why do we have to have this conversation?" Carlos continued. "Why haven't they sold the land yet? Why don't you live in San Fernando with a college degree and a wife by now? Do you think I can keep sending money forever to pay for this? If you do, you're mistaken." He plucked a handful of grass and flung it, but it separated and wafted down softly in the breeze. "None of you appreciate what I'm trying to do." His voice was cold and colored with pain. "It will all be gone one day, pissed away and wasted by people without foresight." He felt his eyes burn, but he bullied the tears back with his rage and then fell silent.

After several seconds his brother stood and nodded again and looked away from his sibling, out into the emerald patchwork at the crooked figure struggling through the mud. "Alright, Carlos," he said finally. "I'll talk to him. You tell us what you want us to do later tonight."

Carlos stood as well, but softened his expression. "I don't mean to be hard about this. But I'm not doing it anymore. I'm not doing it anymore." He shook his head and flicked mud off his t-shirt and then turned and walked back to the house leaving his brother behind him.

That night Carlos sat his family on the rattan couch and ensconced himself in a straight-back wooden chair across from them like a counselor meeting with troubled relatives. He spoke in a patronizing voice of his job and his expenses and of the precarious nature of the economy, and of things they didn't know about like health insurance and 401Ks. His mother nodded and "hmmed" and pretended to understand while his brother fidgeted nervously, watching the old man and smoking a homemade cigarette. His father sat silently with his taunt hands on his knees and listened carefully to each word spoken by his son. The florescent lights hummed and buzzed as insects swarmed in chaotic patterns and made tinkling noises against the thin glass.

"It's time to make a change," Carlos said, finally getting to his point. "We can't go on like this anymore. I've been thinking about this for a long time and its time we made some hard decisions." He shifted in his seat but remained erect. "I'm working and sending money back to try to build a better life for you here, but it doesn't seem to be happening. Nothing seems to be getting any better." He leaned forward with his elbows on his knees and wiped sweat off his forehead with his finger and looked at his parents. "Do you understand? I don't mean to hurt you. It's just not working anymore to keep sinking money into this land." He studied his father and nodded encouragingly, and then took on a stern expression. "You have to sell it," he said in a definitive voice. "You have to sell it or I won't support you anymore. That's the way it's got to be."

The old man looked down and moved his eyes thoughtfully from side to side as if searching for a rebuttal, but there was none to be found. His son's words were etched in stone before he spoke them. He had failed at the only vocation he had ever known. Or perhaps it was the land that had failed him. Deep down he knew that perhaps both were true. His shoulders slumped and his eyes glassed. Somewhere in the darkness a sacred chain as old as the land itself snapped, and its recoil cut the old man in half where he sat. From that point on he was, like his ancestral line of tillers of the earth, broken, though he would not show it. His father let out the breath he was holding and nodded. "All right," he said in an uneven voice, and then he stood and walked out into the blackness.

❧

Carlos's father and brother spent their waking hours in the fields after that, feverishly burying their angst in the mud, laboring under a blistering sun that overwhelmed and purged emotional anguish with physical suffering. Carlos agreed that they should see the current crop cycle through, but after that the land must be sold. He would return to see things through when the time came. With his objective complete, Carlos moved up his departure date to two days hence.

He knew it wouldn't be easy. He felt his brother's anger and bore it like a millstone around his neck. He listened to his arguments and his reasons and his condemnations, but only responded to it with a steadfast determination. His mother sulked and pouted, and withheld her motherly affections, and clucked her tongue, but he ignored it as well. His father was the only one apparently unchanged. He never spoke a word about his son's decision, but simply worked as he had always done. This bothered Carlos most of all. But someone had to make the difficult decisions, he thought. He felt himself an adult among children and despised the dynamic. Why should he be made the bad guy for doing what was necessary? Why should he have to be the voice of reason and prudence? Why did they put him in this position through their gross misunderstanding of a pitiless world? His American wealth seemed more of a curse than a blessing to him. He wished he could just live a normal life like his American friends back in Los Angeles. He couldn't wait to leave the Philippines.

Carlos was asleep in his brother's bed when it happened. It was a deep, tranquilized mid-afternoon tropical sleep; the kind that one sometimes never wakes from. Panicked voices and distant shouts seemed to penetrate the room and echo off the inside of his skull. His mind awakened to a disturbed confusion, but his body continued to lay dormant. He struggled against the lethargy and a rising sense of claustrophobia. Suddenly he was being sucked back down into a soundless void. It covered his eyes and seeped into his lungs. It was coming for him; what, he didn't know, but he was powerless to stop it. He screamed in his mind and his eyes burst opened. The room was hot. His face and body tingled. He shook his head and rubbed his eyes. There was something terribly wrong. He stood and walked out of the house into a seemingly deserted world. Off in the distance he saw a boy running in his direction. Desperate and out of breath, the young man's skinny arms and legs flailed as he stumbled into a forward lean. When he reached Carlos he stood heaving with his hands on his knees, and wagged his head back and forth. "It's your father," he said in between gasps. "Something has happened."

Carlos took the boy by the shoulders and stood him up straight. "What has happened to my father?"

The boy shook his head. "I don't know. I couldn't see. They told me to come get you."

Carlos let him go and set off in a sprint across the earthen yard and out into the great expanse of rice fields. He ran in his bare feet along the embankments, twisting and balancing and leaping to cut corners. The world seemed to be devoid of people as he searched for the source of the shouts and terrible cries that had awakened him, but there was nothing. He searched for his mother as well, but she was nowhere to be seen. Soon he could discern them in the distance. His brother was bent over, his elbows hooked under his father's armpits as he struggled through the mud. He took great, high steps and then fell backward pulling his father on top of him as he became submerged the silty mess. He struggled and splashed and stood again and continued to drag his father out of the pit. He called out the name of God in desperation and cried anguished sobs. Carlos raced, stumbling and splashing frantically as the delicate dyke crumbled along the edges under his furious pace.

When he came upon them the old man lay on a grassy embankment with his brother wiping the mud from his father's face and calling out his name. Carlos fell to his knees and bent low over the ancient farmer. The old man's eyes fluttered wildly as he gasped out breathy, imperceptible words. "I'm here, papa,"

Carlos said, gripping his father's withered, gritty, mud-covered hand around the thumb pad. "I'm here." His father's eyes calmed at the voice and eventually they settled on Carlos's face. He looked at his son for a long while and then smiled softly the way a father does when his son performs a good deed that he can be proud of. Carlos sobbed out apologies. "I'm sorry, papa. I'm so sorry." The old man's eyes shifted upward and glassed over as he searched for the words that would never come. And then he gave up the ghost, his heart broken inside his chest.

Carlos laid his head on his father and wept bitterly into the drying mud. The old man lay still, his spirit departed and his body destined to become part of the very earth that he so loved, and which his son so despised.

❧

My Lolo doesn't come anymore. No one visits me now. The fields and the trees and the stilted houses in the tropical sun are all gone. There is nothing left but a barren and ash-colored wilderness without sun, or light, or humanity. I stumble through it calling my father's name, but I know he is not there. He is standing in the emerald patchwork of eternity watching the golden rice stalks bow and dance in the breeze. He sees the earth regenerate again and again, and stands with the fertile ground in between his toes and nods approvingly at the bounty laid out before him. I know I have no part with him, and so I sit in the blackness and wait for the dream to end. What more can I do?

The American Road Home

Emilio lay silently in his bed listening to the commotion above him. His grandchildren were up and plodding about their morning routines. He heard the reluctant thumps of a teenage boy and the irregular pattering of the younger ones scrambling across the floor, the clank of dishes and the peculiar yammering of cartoon characters from the television. It was all so oddly foreign to him. He should have been up hours ago, before everyone else, but there was no point to it that he could see; no animals to feed, no plants to tend to, no warm pandesal to buy, nothing but the cold sterile Chicago morning to greet him. He lay flat on his back with his arms stacked on his chest. There hadn't been anyone to touch beside him for almost eight years now. He shifted under the weight of the quilt and tented it with his feet. He'd slept with nothing more than a thin bed sheet for the past seventy-four years of his life and he missed the lightness of it. He missed a lot of things, but one's options decline as they age; as the world evolves beyond them and leaves them standing as relics of undoubtedly simpler times. His son, Joseph, was insistent that he migrate. He had been petitioning for it for the past six years. It's hard for an only son to observe his filial devotions from ten thousand miles, and so he takes care of his father the best way he knows how.

Emilio unstacked his hands and placed them down along side his torso and pressed on the soft mattress. It pressed back more than he expected. He shifted and then peeled back the covers. The cold immediately lay on him like a wet towel and he pulled the blankets back. It was a difficult decision to rise, but eventually he did. He stood for a few seconds in his blue striped pajamas and then put on his house slippers and slowly ascended the stairs while holding the banister for balance.

He peered into the kitchen unnoticed. The young ones sat slurping their cereal from metal spoons while arguing about words printed on a rectangular box. The teenager was already gone, or never came down. He was a busy boy, smart and athletic, fully Americanized and going places in this competitive society. Emilio shuffled in and pulled out a chair and sat down amidst the clutter. The two children, a boy of ten and a girl of seven, looked up from their breakfasts and greeted the old man in unison, "Good morning, Lolo." He smiled back at them and asked about their breakfast but they didn't understand his question and they giggled amongst themselves. He shrugged and smiled, and then just watched them eat.

Soon there was another more urgent pattering of steps as his is daughter-in-law Noreen hustled into the kitchen. "Good morning, Tay," she greeted. She was already dressed in her powder blue scrubs and had her hair back in a tight ponytail. She chided the children for being so slow and then studied a calendar held to the fridge with a magnet. "Do you want some coffee or toast?" she asked, still looking at the paper calendar.

The old man looked around the kitchen and tucked his chilled hands under his armpits. "I'll have some coffee I think. I need something warm to hold."

Noreen turned and smiled and pulled a cup from its brass hook, and then poured the coffee black and handed it to Emilio. He held it with both hands like a priceless gem, lifting it just under his chin but not taking a drink. He held it that way for a long while, smelling it and thinking about what the day might hold while the hurricane of activity swirled around him. The children finished their breakfasts and left their bowls where they sat, still a quarter full of yellowish milk with bits of floating cereal settling along the parameter. Noreen chided them again and shooed them out of the room toward the door. "Don't worry about any of this," she advised Emilio, shaking her head. "I'll take care of it later." And then he sat alone. Shouts and arguments rang out and then died and ignited again. Someone couldn't find a shoe, another a backpack. Joseph tramped down the stairs in his white shirt and blazer and rushed to his car without a goodbye, shouting something to the kids as he negotiated the icy steps. Noreen called out announcing their departure and estimating when they might to be back. She told him to just take it easy and again not to worry about anything. The children called out in unison, "Goodbye, Lolo," and then all three left and closed the door and there was quiet throughout the house.

Emilio sipped at his coffee, pulling his legs close together against the cold from the recently opened door. He listened to a clock ticking softly. Something hummed low and continuous from behind the pantry door. He shifted in his seat and it seemed to make a tremendous noise as it creaked. He sat with his elbows on the table holding his coffee and staring out a sliding glass door into the bleak morning unfolding over the city. He thought of his family and of his wife, and wondered how the rest of his life would turn out in this place, but it was impossible to tell. And so he turned his thoughts to home and recalled older times.

Emilio turned the silver knob one way and then the other. Then he turned the other knob to the left and corrected it and then turned it left again. It was impossible. The water came out ice cold or unbearably hot, and neither was something he could stand in for five to seven minutes. He turned them both off and sat on the edge of the tub like a mechanic trying to diagnose engine trouble. He felt silly even though it was just him there. They had showed him how the shower worked many times, but it was difficult to get right. Finally he pulled up the stopper and let the water run hot into the bathtub, figuring that he'd just let it cool before he got in.

He went through his clothes while he waited. There was nothing of his own to wear except for a pair of knock-off Levis he'd bought in Manila. He pulled them off the shelf and stacked one of his son's gray sweatshirts on top, and then set the pile on the bed with a pair of socks to the side. It was going to be a cold day.

When it cooled he lay in the water for a long time staring at the ceiling. The water was warm and felt good, but the empty house was unnerving. He laved the water over his hair and forehead and the drops splashed musically in the tub. He would stop occasionally and listen, sure he heard a door creak open or footsteps on the floor above him or voices talking soft and low, but there was nothing. He continued his bath until he thought he heard them again and then he sat frozen in the silence. Finally he gave up and pushed down the stopper and listened as the water gurgled down the pipes.

Emilio dressed quickly and combed his thinning hair to the side while it was still damp. His body shook from the chill and he tried to calm it by rubbing his arms in an embrace, but it brought no warmth. He brushed his teeth and put on his slippers and climbed the stairs again where the air seemed slightly warmer. He walked slowly through the living room and marveled again at his son's many possessions, at the clutter. Every variety of electronics with their tangled wires and dull red lights, cushioned furniture flanked by end tables and coffee tables, all covered with magazines and glasses and schoolbooks and graded assignments beset with stickers and giant "OKs." He examined a china hutch filled with mismatched curios and geometric crystal gems that served no purpose at all. Nothing from his homeland. He then wandered into the kitchen and ate a plain piece of bread while sitting at the table. He sat for a long time until he couldn't stand it anymore and then rose and gathered up the dishes and washed each one in the sink and set them out to dry. He didn't put them in the dishwasher, he didn't trust it. It took hands and scrubbing and careful inspection to make sure a dish was clean and no machine could do that. He washed other dishes too, scouring the house for stray glasses and plates. He then wiped the table and the counter and organized everything just so until he felt comfortable enough to sit, but he didn't feel like resting, and so he walked back to the living room and cleaned it too. He spent most of the morning this way, straitening and organizing, cleaning and polishing. It wasn't proper work for an old farmer like him, but it was productive and he felt like he was earning his keep. They would be upset with him for troubling himself, but they didn't have time to stay upset for too long, their lives were much too busy.

By the time he was finished it was already noon. He turned on the TV, but couldn't discern the buttons on either the set or the remote. He pressed a few and the screen went blue. He pressed a few more but nothing changed. He then turned the set off and sat back to listen to the quiet again. They wouldn't be home for another six hours. And then what? Dinner, homework, laundry, TV, some friendly chat and then off to bed to start the routine all over again. He despaired at the endless cycle and idly wondered how long he had left to live on this earth. It was a morbid thought and he knew it, but there was also something strangely pleasant about it. It couldn't go on forever.

After attempting a nap and frying some rice left in the cooker in oil and soy sauce, Emilio decided to venture outside. He peeked out the window and gazed at the sky, everything gray. He pulled on a puffy red coat and tugged a stocking cap over the crown of his head. He didn't feel immediately warmer like he thought he would. It was a strange, cloistered feeling inside the coat and hat, like a moth must feel in its cocoon, he thought. He slipped his feet into a pair of galoshes and then opened the door and walked out into the cold. The frigid air struck him at once and his face tensed and pulsed like it had been slapped. He stood on the front stoop surveying the ground before him. The slushy snow lay in winding skiffs across the yard. Waves of grass lay bent over, pressed flat by the melted weight, and then stood erect again like great untamed cowlicks. A sharp wind cut along the front of the house and whistled by, causing the evergreen bushes to quake erratically. Emilio shrugged his shoulders and nestled his ears inside the coat's collar. He felt like he should leave the stoop, but where to? He didn't trust the icy walkway. He looked up and down the street. Not a soul. Empty driveways and plantation blinds drawn as far as the eye could see. It seemed as if this affluent suburb had been suddenly struck by an epidemic disease, purging the inhabitants to a person. He shifted his weight to one foot and then the other, bouncing softly for warmth, but soon he felt silly standing there in the cold and he went back inside.

Out of ideas, he lay on the couch flipping though magazines until he heard a car pull in just after 6pm.

Days and then weeks passed by with little change. The weather remained cold. He tried to become acquainted with his family, but they remained strangers. He seemed to inhabit an odd limbo, observing life curiously from somewhere outside of it. Sometimes he even saw himself within this observable reality, but he was lifeless and waxen like a statue in a museum that neither spoke nor acted in a lifelike way, and soon it became too much.

"I want to go back to the Philippines," he told his son one evening during an episode of "American Idol." "I want to go home."

Joseph paused the DVR and shifted, facing his father. He studied him for a moment. "What? Why? I thought you were enjoying it here."

The old man pursed his lips and blinked thoughtfully while Noreen and the kids separated in various directions to allow the awkward conversation to play out. "I enjoy being close to you and the family," he explained, "but there's nothing for me to do here."

Joseph shook his head. "That's the point, isn't it? You're in retirement now. You worked hard all your life and now you get to rest. That's how life is supposed to be. You're just not used to it yet. It will take time for you to get accustomed to it." He patted his father's knee sympathetically. "There would be no rest for you in the Philippines. Mama is dead. What would you do there?"

Emilio considered his son's question carefully. He didn't know what he would do, but it wouldn't be nothing. At least he wouldn't be trapped in a cold empty house. "I'd go back to my life, I guess."

Joseph chuckled. "Your life? What is that? Who would take care of you? What if you got sick? I can't just jump on a plane any time and come to the Philippines, you know." He leaned back against a checkered cushion and shook his head again. "It just wouldn't work. It's not possible. I love you, Papa. We all love you and we want you here with us."

The old man sighed deeply and squinted at his son. How could he tell him of his misery? How could he explain his inexplicable desire to return to the land of his birth? What was it about the Philippines that drew him back? Familiarity? The weather? No. It was something more, something intangible; something that defied any single context. It wasn't a thing or a person or a single quality, it was a way of life, a means of existing. It was something real, a life he would inhabit rather than merely observe from the outside. "Well, I want to go back," was his only reply.

Joseph drew a breath and exhaled it slowly. "I understand, Papa, but it just can't happen. Not now, anyway. We spent all our savings to get you here and we can't afford another ticket right now. Maybe next fall." He smiled and patted his father's knee again. "But I bet by then you won't want to leave." He shifted among the cushions and hit the play button on the remote. The crowd cheered and a contestant took the stage. Joseph called to the rest of the family and they filtered in from various directions, their eyes set on the television while Emilio sank back into the abyss of his disappointment.

❧

Emilio's days dragged and bled into one another, all the same. He'd taken to watching Tagalog movies, but quickly grew bored of them. The weather remained cold into February and he rarely ventured outside. The house was quiet and foreign, never increasing in familiarity or warmth. He walked the halls and inhabited the rooms like a patient in a hospital, waiting for some miracle recovery, calling the doctors by their titles instead of their names and smiling hollowly at the nurses.

One afternoon, however, he was seized upon by some strange motivation. He dressed in his coat and stocking cap and pulled a pair of white cotton gloves over his hands and galoshes on his feet. He then rose and set off inexplicably down the street toward the low hanging midday sun without locking the house behind him. He walked aimlessly in the cold and the wind, tucking his face in his coat and lowering his chin to divert the breeze. He passed silent houses and empty parks, structures and places that hummed of desolation. He veered left at a T in the road and walked on, unconcerned with how he might find his way back. The cold was brutal, but he walked on nonetheless. Off in the distance he caught sight of cars on a cross street. Traffic lights beamed and then died and the vehicles raced and halted accordingly. Beyond the crossing there was a large storefront with the words "Jewel Osco" in red across the front. He recognized the enterprise from shopping trips with Noreen. The parking lot had less than a dozen cars but was littered with shopping carts. A lonely patron hastily tossed grocery bags in the back of an SUV to escape the cold. Emilio walked until he reached the street, and then he crossed it and traversed the parking lot and entered the establishment, stomping his feet as he passed through the electric doors.

The store was quiet except for soft music coming from the ceiling. Stock boys and other employees milled about, placing products or sweeping portions of the floor with a broad swivel broom. Emilio stood just inside the door surveying the layout before him. He didn't have a dime to his name but ventured among the wares anyway, strolling up and down the aisles casually examining the products with his hands in his coat pockets. He spent a long time in the meager hardware section studying various tools and trying to calculate their prices in pesos.

After more than an hour he walked up to the customer service desk and placed his bony hands on the counter. A heavy-set man with a mustache and a red apron turned and greeted him cheerfully. "Hello sir, what can I do for you?"

Emilio nodded at him and bid him a formal "good day" in English. The pair then looked at each other for several awkward seconds. The fat man twisted slightly on his heel and smiled and let out a small burst of air through his nose. "Is there something I can help you with? Are you looking for something?"

Emilio lowered his eyes, but raised them again immediately and looked directly into the manager's round face. "I'm looking for work," he said, feeling the weight of his accent.

The manager lost his smile, but studied the old man thoughtfully. "Really? Why are you looking for work?"

The old man pointed at himself and then off into the distance. "I need money to go home. I am a Pilipino."

The manager puckered his lips to one side and hung his hands in an apron pocket and regarded the old man curiously for a long while. "Do you have papers?"

Emilio lifted his hands from the counter and shuffled in his stance. "I have papers," he said as confidently as possible. "I am an immigration visa." The English didn't sound right, but he let it hang.

"Do you have a social security number?"

Emilio shook his head.

"How about a work permit? A green card?"

The old man shook his head again and let his eyes fall down.

The manager wiped his finger across his mustache several times and squinted one eye. "What kind of work can you do?"

Emilio looked up. "I can do many work. I'm strong. I'm old, but I'm strong." He clenched two fists to punctuate his point. "I can do anything in this place."

The manager smiled. "I see. Well, that's just it. I don't need you to do anything in this place. I need someone to collect carts in the parking lot and stack them inside the entryway. Do you know what I mean?

Emilio nodded enthusiastically. "Yes, I know."

"You can do that?

"Yes, I can do that."

"It's cold out there. You have to keep at it. You can't quit and come inside. Do you understand? I need someone I can depend on."

"Yes. Yes, I understand."

The manager folded his arms across his chest and stared silently for several long seconds cocking his head one way and then the other. "All right then," he said finally, "you can start today." He nodded definitively at Emilio, half expecting him to get to work, but the old man stood fast.

"How much did you paid me?" he asked, one eye half-squinted.

The manager scratched his neck for a moment and sized up the old man carefully. "How about $5.00 an hour?"

Emilio quickly calculated the amount into pesos, almost 250, a tremendous amount; but his airline ticket wouldn't cost pesos, it would cost dollars. The old man looked up and exhaled and dimpled his hollow cheeks skeptically; gestures he had perfected over years of negotiation in markets and feed stores in the Philippines. "I want six," he declared.

The manager smiled more broadly and then let out a chuckle. "All right, you got it. I'll pay you each Friday in cash. Just write your hours on a piece of paper each day when you're done, all right? Now get to work."

Emilio nodded and turned, digging in his pockets for the white cotton gloves as he made for the door. The sun hung pale in the southwest and a sharp wind continued to blow. The parking lot was less than a quarter full. Shopping carts stood scattered over the whole of it, a half dozen or more wedged into a large mound of snow to keep from rolling away. Emilio pulled his stocking cap down and marched out onto the black top. He struggled with the carts one by one in the slush, banging them against the cement and stacking them horizontally in the elongated vestibule. His hands were numb and his jaw and ears ached terribly. He stopped occasionally, wheezing in the burning cold, his breath a white plume in the gray afternoon. Within an hour he had cleared the parking lot and stood shivering on the sidewalk watching for customers. The late afternoon brought an increase in traffic and soon the lot stood half full. He lurked among the parked cars, seizing on abandoned carts and halting before the moving vehicles while customers regarded him warily as they would a vagrant.

Eventually the gray celestial orb dipped below the horizon and Emilio knew it was approaching five o'clock. He entered the store and made his way back to the customer service desk where he searched for the manager, but he wasn't there. He surveyed the counter for familiar papers and looked back and forth at the checkout stations. Finally he moved down the counter and pushed past a waist-high swinging door. He shuffled through some random papers, but found nothing.

"Hey, what do you think you are doing?" Emilio snapped up and stared wide-eyed at a young woman in a red vest. She wore a severe scowl that caused a golden ring in her eyebrow to stand on end. "Who do you think you are?"

Emilio stammered and quivered his head. "I'm working the carts. It's my job now. Today. I want to write my hours."

Her scowl softened but didn't disappear. "Oh, you must be the one Marv told me about. Well, he didn't leave you a time sheet. Just tell me your hours and I can write it down."

Emilio made a pained face and shook his head. "I want to write my hours please. He told me to write them."

The girl's scowl returned in full as she sighed and pushed behind the counter to fish out a blank time sheet from a cubbyhole. "We don't really use these any more, but put your name on it and then the date and how many hours you worked and pin it here when you're done." She tapped her black fingernail on a corkboard scattered with papers.

Emilio picked up a pen chained to the counter and scribbled out the information and pinned it neatly to the corkboard as instructed. He looked up at the girl, now standing next to a cash register with her arms folded. "Thank you," he said. She shrugged and nodded and stood there rigidly until he was well on his way out of the store and into the evening chill.

ஃ

It only took Emilio a matter of days to become expert at his new work. He waited every morning for his family to go their separate ways and then he bundled up and bustled off under the iron sky toward the Jewel Osco, treading the snow strewn sidewalks and eyeing the traffic with caution. The cold remained bitter and agonizing, but he discovered ways to ward it off. He would stomp his feet and rub his hands, or ball them up in the palms of his white cotton gloves and squeeze them under his armpits. He would sometimes linger in the blasts of warm air coming through the automatic sliding doors or purchase a cup of coffee and hold it gingerly while he waited for carts to accumulate. Soon he became indifferent to the weather and simply accepted it as a part of the job.

He continued gathering the baskets one at a time and stacking them neatly inside the vestibule, and took tremendous pride in the neatness of a cartless parking lot when he was done. It felt good to work, to strain and struggle for compensation, no matter how meager. It is what he knew, what he was cut out for, and what he would do until he died.

Each day he would pass silently inside the store and mark his hours and post them on the board where they remained undisturbed until the next day. Each Friday the hefty manager would pat him on the shoulder and tell him what a good job he was doing and hand him a plain envelope containing that week's salary — $200, sometimes more. He thanked him at each encounter and folded the envelope and put it in his front pocket. He always waited until he was home to count it, and then he would stuff it in a small box and hide it in a dresser drawer. His family knew nothing of his work. They scarcely noticed any change in him at all. He smiled at their ignorance, and feigned boredom in the evenings and complained about the long cold days alone. It made him feel like a naughty teenager sneaking around behind his parents back and he liked the thrill of it.

Winter slowly passed into the early stages of spring and the sky became sunnier, a crystal china blue chilled by the March winds. The great mounds of plowed snow in the parking lot melted into dirty slurry and then disappeared altogether, leaving winding forms of sediment in their absence. Patrons unhurried by the milder weather began to acknowledge Emilio in their comings and goings. They waved and spoke to him and learned his name, and he came to know them as well; old women with time to talk, frazzled mothers piling grocery bags into their trunks, college students on beer runs, and workers purchasing their boxed lunches from the deli. They all smiled and thanked him genuinely when he took their carts like a valet, and marveled at his fortitude. "I hope I have your stamina when I'm your age," they would say. "That's the kind of work that made America great. I hope the young ones are watching you." Some gave him tips. Others wanted to shake his hand and have their children take a good look at a real worker, as they told the gaping youngsters of similar jobs they had worked in their earlier days. Soon he gained a reputation around the neighborhood and people sought him out. There was something genuine and inspiring about him and they told him so. "It does me good to see you," they would say. "You're a good man. We need more people like you. You're not afraid to roll up your sleeves and work."

It seemed so strange to Emilio that he should be considered the American ideal. After all, he was working for his ticket home. He laughed internally and shook his head at the Americans' fascination with work that they would never do. He marveled at their nostalgia and scoffed at their dramatic praise of his mundane tasks. It was as if they were looking into a golden past, an America beyond the grasp of their temporal positions; one that they longed for but could not—or would not—recapture themselves, but were content to see embodied in this old man.

It was strange to him. Nevertheless, he came to love them too and appreciated their ideals as they appreciated his work.

❧

By the end of May, Emilio had amassed over $3500 and stashed it away in his dresser drawer. On a sunny Tuesday morning after the family was all gone, he split the money into two piles and folded each over and then stuffed it in his front pockets. He looked up a cab company in the yellow pages and called it and then stood outside until the car arrived, basking in the warmth.

"Where to?" asked the driver, studying the old man in the rearview mirror. His accent was heavy. Emilio had hoped he was Filipino at first glance, but he wasn't. He was Lebanese.

"I'll go to O'Hare airport, please."

The driver knit his brow in confusion. "You don't have any bags."

"I know."

"You travel without bags?"

"I'm not traveling."

"Oh, you go to pick someone up? I can wait, you know."

Emilio settled back without buckling his seatbelt. "No. No. It's ok. I'm just buy a ticket to the Philippines."

The driver continued staring. "You want to buy a ticket? At the airport? That's no good."

Emilio heaved a sigh. "I'm just want to buy a ticket to the Philippines. I'm going home. Can you take me?"

The driver shook his head and then nodded to complete the asymmetry of their conversation, and pulled off down the road toward O'Hare International Airport. He continued chirping advice on buying tickets online, but Emilio ignored him. It wasn't terribly far to O'Hare and Emilio paid the man with a twenty and thanked him. The driver wished him good luck and shook his head one more time, and then drove away amid the throng of halting vehicles.

The terminal was bustling with travelers. He looked warily at the men in dark business suits shouting at their cell phones and curiously regarded the families huddled together around their luggage with the young ones sitting on the upright bags. There was a sports team milling around, all dressed alike and laughing and shoving each other with their luggage sprawled out across the floor. Emilio stood back from the crowds and scanned the signs for a familiar carrier. His eyes eventually fell on a Northwest Airline logo that he recognized it from his original voyage.

It took forty minutes to reach the desk, where Emilio was greeted by a chipper-middle aged woman with dark curly hair. "Where are we traveling today, sir?"

The old man placed his hands on the counter amidst a chaotic smattering of blank luggage tags. "I need to buy a ticket to the Philippines, please." The woman opened her mouth and then closed it and frowned and shook her head the way the cab driver did.

"You want to buy a ticket?"

"Yes, please."

The woman eyed the line of passengers behind the old man and shook her head again. "I see. Well, um, can you hold on a second?" The woman stepped away and a ripple of irritated murmurs spread through the line. A child began to cry. Emilio stood rigid with his hands still on the counter and his eyes straight ahead. After several uncomfortable minutes the woman returned with a beautiful young Filipina. "Sir, I think this woman can help you." The beautiful woman smiled at Emilio and spoke to him gently in Tagalog and asked him if he'd like to step aside and talk.

They walked slowly together as he told her everything; about his migration, his family, his job at the Jewel Osco, his loneliness, the cold weather, and his desperate desire to return home. He was surprised by his own forthrightness and laughed and marveled at his own story as he told it, suddenly so exceptional and improbable. The Filipina listened silently, save gentle encouragements and she teared inexplicably at his words.

"I want to help you," she said, placing her hand on his shoulder. "I want to get you home."

She explained to him how he could buy a ticket on the internet, but he shook his head midway through. "I don't have a computer, or a credit card. And the only computer I know of is my son's. I can't do that."

The Filipina frowned. "Then how were you going to pay for it?"

Emilio dug in his pockets and pulled out the cash, holding it precariously in both hands. "There's over three thousand here."

The Filipina looked at the ragged pile and smiled. "I think we can work something out."

She took him to a small office where a laptop computer hummed softly on a Formica counter. "Let's get you a ticket. I'll just book it on my credit card and you can pay me."

Emilio crumpled his face and made an uncertain sound. "I'd like to buy it."

The Filipina patted his arm softly. "You will be buying it, from me, I guess. I'd like to sell you a ticket. You can pay me in cash. All right?"

Emilio studied her carefully and then nodded and smiled.

They sat together going over various itineraries and prices until Emilio settled on a one-way flight for $976. The Filipina paid and Emilio counted out a thousand dollars in tens, twenties and hundreds and handed it to her in a neat pile. "Many thanks," he said, gripping one of her hands with both of his. She smiled and teared again and hugged him close, like she would her own grandfather. He embraced her back and basked in the kinship between them.

A printer creaked and buzzed somewhere behind them and then stopped. The Filipina retrieved three pieces of paper, stapled them and then handed them to Emilio. "Here you go. Everything is ready to go."

The old man looked confused. "When do I get my ticket?"

She moved in beside him to look at the papers together. "This is your ticket. They have you in the computer. All you have to do is check in with your passport and these numbers will tell them you're on this flight." She ran her delicate finger along a series of numbers and tapped the paper softly. "It's all right here."

He nodded uncertainly and then finally smiled his approval. If he couldn't trust this angel then who could he trust? He thanked her again and she hugged him once more and walked him out to a long line of cabs. She then wished him luck and stood on the sidewalk until he rolled out of sight, waving all the while.

Emilio reveled in his victory on the ride home, telling the cab driver, a black man this time, the details of his saga. The driver smiled and listened carefully, and told of his own desire to get back to Florida where he was from. The trip was quick, and Emilio gladly overpaid again. He wished the driver good luck in his endeavor and then hustled inside to complete the charade of his lonely day. He was eager to tell his family about the ticket. They would be upset certainly, but they had to admire him, for his fortitude and resourcefulness, for his ability to achieve such an improbable goal after only a few months in this foreign land. Yes, they would have to admire him.

He waited for the right time to tell them, but no right time appeared. Dinner was hectic, every person eating at their own pace and in their own seat in the living room, scanning the news for weather and then watching a reality show where contestants danced for the approval of judges. When the show finished, Emilio raised his voice as one might expect from a patriarch. The family fell silent and regarded him curiously. He leaned forward with his elbows on his knees and nodded at their silence. "I'm going home next month," he stated in Tagalog. The children squinted and strained to understand the thinly familiar language while Joseph sighed and shook his head. Emilio continued, "I've enjoyed staying with you. You are my family and families should spend time together, but I need to go home. I won't forget you though, and you are welcome to come see me any time."

Joseph waved his hands back and forth as if to dispel the words like smoke. He spoke Tagalog now as well and the kids turned back to the television, though it was muted. "Papa, we've been through this before. Your place is here now. We spent so much money to get you here and we don't have enough for you to go back. Do you understand?"

Emilio dug in his back pocket and fished out a neatly fold stack of papers. He unfolded the itinerary and handed it to Joseph. "It's already done. I'm leaving for sure. I took care of everything. I earned the money. I bought the ticket."

Joseph studied the names and numbers and cities and dates and flipped through the pages one by one and furrowed his brow and frowned at the ink. "How could you do this? How could you do this to me, to us?" He looked critically at his father with accusing eyes. Though they did not fully understand the exchange, the children quietly gathered their dishes and exited the room in silence. "I brought you here to take care of you. I sacrificed so you could live out your life in comfort with your family." Joseph ruffled his hair in frustration. "You don't care about any of it. You never gave it a chance. You wanted to leave the moment you arrived and never stopped to think about what was best. Do you know how many people would give anything to be in your place? Do you have any idea how difficult it is to immigrate to America?"

Emilio steeled his jaw and glared at his son. "Don't forget who it is you're talking to, boy. I'm not one of your kids and I'm not some ignorant immigrant either. I made my way in this country and now I'm making my way back. You must respect that."

Joseph exhaled and slumped his shoulders in defeat. His father was right. He wasn't a child, and perhaps he wasn't in need of care like a child either. He threw his hands up dramatically. "All right," he conceded. "All right. You've made your decision. I wish you would stay, but it's your money and you can do what you want with it. If you don't want to be with your family, then that's just fine."

Emilio grimaced and cupped his hand around the back of his son's neck. "I'm still good, son," he said, his voice strong but gentle. "Still strong. I shouldn't be sitting around waiting to die. It's not what I'm cut out for. You should know that about your own father. It's what I taught you. I've got land and a house in the Philippines. I've got over two-thousand dollars in my pocket. That's a lot in the provinces; as much as I'll need. Don't worry about me. I'll be fine. I always have been fine."

Joseph heaved a breath and then nodded. His eyes welled slightly, from guilt or pride he couldn't tell, and so he rubbed them with his thumb and forefinger to hide it. Emilio shook his son's shoulder to dispel the uncomfortable emotion. "Besides," he teased, "now that I'm a rich *balik-bayan* maybe I'll hire a pretty young maid to take care of me."

Joseph laughed at his father's irreverence and looked sincerely at the old man. "Now you're making sense." And there was admiration hidden in his eyes.

Emilio labored his last day at the Jewel Osco under an unseasonably hot sun. Nevertheless, he still worked in blue jeans, a long sleeved tee-shirt, and a beige military-style bucket hat on his head. He was happy in his work and would miss it when he was gone. The patrons called him by name and greeted him happily. He returned their waves, but spoke nothing of his impending departure. Soon he would be gone, vanished from their frantic lives like the nostalgic memories he evoked in them. They would pause, pondering for a melancholy moment when they discovered his absence, but soon other distractions would take his place and his time among them would fade. He knew it to be true and he liked the anonymity of it.

"So it's your last day, huh?" Marv stood behind the customer service counter in his red apron just as he did on the first day he and Emilio met. "I'm going to be sorry to see you go. We all are."

Emilio looked up from his time sheet and smiled. "Thank you for the job, sir. I very much enjoy working here."

The manager nodded and rubbed his mustache with his forefinger, and then dug in his apron pocket for a moment. When his hand emerged it bore a small bulging envelope. He handed it to Emilio. "This is for you," he said.

Emilio held it gingerly in his hands and studied it like a puzzle box, but said nothing.

"Well, open it!" boomed the hefty manager. "You should open it now."

Emilio carefully tore up the pasted flap and peered inside. It was filled with a half inch of stacked cash, twenties and tens, fives and ones all wrinkled and nicked, laying next to one another in silent order. Next to the sack was a long white card. Emilio fished it out and examined the front. "We Will Miss You," it read in staggered columns and fancy blue script. Inside he found a tumultuous collection of well wishes and signatures from his fellow employees. He read through them in silence, names he only faintly recognized and short-hand messages he didn't fully understand, punctuated by exclamation points and smiley faces. He marveled at their abundance and their intimacy, and at the baffling significance of an insignificant person. Finally, he nodded quietly at the card and ran the heel of his hand along his cheek. "Thank you, sir."

Marv smiled and shook his hand across the counter. "You're a good man, Emilio. You take care of yourself."

Emilio woke in the early morning on his split-wood rattan bed and lay quietly in the cool morning air. There was no sound but that common to the daybreak, and he reveled in the mundane silence of it. This day was his, his to work and watch and to tread the ground of his homeland wherever he chose. He thought of his family on the other side of the world and smiled at them and wished them happiness. They were far away, but he knew the road well now. He thought of his journey and grinned. Then he just lay soundless. And time passed not at all save for the gradual movement of the tropical sun.

Epilogue

Bereaved and hapless, he stands in the rain like a fool, watching the great metal machine idle in the downpour. She turns to look with her almond eye, casting her gaze through the streaked window to where the rain has mingled with his tears. His breath is forced from his body by some primeval power, like an accursed person witnessing the departing of a soul from its body. He is the last to see her living, and he, the first visage of her estranged spirit. The machine rolls forward, creeping into the foreboding distance. Overcome with panic and regret, she presents her full face as a parting gesture and places a desperate hand on the glass. Still the machine rolls, displacing pooled water and breaking a path through the storm. The angle grows narrower and she presses more desperately against the pane until he becomes invisible. Her world falls silent except for the tapping of the rain and the low rumble of the machine. And still he stands in the rain like a fool, bereaved and hapless.

Acknowledgements

It would be an understatement to say that I was uneasy about delving into the world of fiction writing. I've spent many years training myself to be an academic writer, and continue to enjoy it as my primary occupation. The thrill of the archival search, the sequence of the logic, the discovery of lost worlds and unknown characters, and the contentious debates of historical inquiry fill me with unspeakable pleasures. And yet, amidst all of this excitement there was and is something still lacking—something lurking just beyond the methodologies and archival evidence, something unreachable and elusive about the human condition that formal studies can't capture. I'm still not sure what that something is, but these stories are my attempt to discover it. For me, this book represents a frontier of strange explorations. It represents my curious inquiry into the metaphysical nature of our existence—the unquantifiable qualities that craft our notions of ourselves, and others, and of the world. It is my effort to artistically interpret a small piece of humanity, and I hope it serves a purpose.

Given these insecurities, I was somewhat hesitant at first to circulate the above stories. After some time, however, I began to release them to immediate family members and solicit their criticisms. In this regard, I owe a deep debt of gratitude to my mother, Sandra Hawkins, whose love of literature and keen eyes offered the first significant critiques of this project. Our lengthy discussions and resulting insights helped to polish and refine the tales I meant to share. Soon enough my father, Carey Hawkins, was also involved. His comments were shorter and more pointed, but their subtle honesty stewed in my mind and prompted many revisions.

I also owe thanks to my sister, Jessica Sharp, whose love of classic literature brought many severe and starkly honest critiques to this work. Her comments, almost always prefaced with a "don't take this the wrong way" or "I hope this doesn't hurt your feelings," significantly shaped my selection and revision of the stories in this volume. I sincerely appreciated her honest approach.

Similarly, I want to express gratitude to my brother, Jeremiah, whose long hours serving his country in Iraq left him ample time to thoroughly read my work. I appreciated his insights on the characters, themes, and story selection for the final manuscript. Mostly, however, I appreciated our profound conversations on the subjects this book attempts to address—life, love, pain, and the way things ought to be.

Last, but certainly not least, I want to extend profound gratitude to my wife, Eve, who, as a member of the diaspora I seek to explore, offered an endless supply of insights, experiences, and corrections to the above work. And also to my children, Isaac and Mika, who have come with us on many adventures to the Philippines and lived their young lives in the crucible of my research. Thank you so much.

Let me also extend sincere thanks to those who took interest in this project near its completion. To Rosemary Sneeringer and Philip Cerepak, whose deft eye and literary sense added invaluable insights and corrections to the manuscript; to Pam Knight and the staff at Plain View Press for their continued efforts; and, of course, to the late Susan Bright, whose initial interest in and reading of this manuscript set it firmly on the path to publication. Thank you all.

Finally, let me offer my sincerest gratitude to the thousands of Filipinos who have provided the magic in my life. Your struggles and triumphs, genius and flaws, compelling culture and unequalled kindness have provided me with a thousand inspirations and a thousand aspirations. Thank you from the bottom of my heart.

Discussion Guide

1. How does globalization effect social relationship in these stories?

- Are the effects of globalization felt more acutely in Diaspora communities? Why?
- Are the opportunities of a globalized world ultimately worth the hardships and sacrifice?

2. How does the author portray power and agency in these stories?

- Are any characters true victims?
- How do the characters exercise their power and agency in a variety of contexts?
- Is there heroism and villainy found in the mundane moments of the lives described in these stories?

3. What is the extent of one's familial obligations?

- Do the characters in these stories faithfully fulfill their obligations to family members?
- Do any fail in their obligations? Why?

About the Author

Michael Hawkins is a professor of Asian History at Creighton University. He currently lives in Omaha with his wife, Eve, and children, Isaac and MikaElla. Michael's research interests range from imperialism and Islam in Southeast Asia, to language, to historiography in Modern China. He has authored numerous articles on the above subjects, and is the author or co-author of the following forth-coming books, *Filipino Verb Guide* (with Rhodalyn Gallo-Crail) (Northern Illinois University Press), *Filipino Tapestry: Language Through Culture* (with Rhodalyn Gallo-Crail) (University of Wisconsin Press), and *Making Moros* (Northern Illinois University Press).

www.ingramcontent.com/pod-product-compliance
Lightning Source LLC
Chambersburg PA
CBHW071019180726
48291CB00004B/1535

* 9 7 8 1 9 3 5 5 1 4 9 1 6 *